DRAGON'S GIFT

DRAGON'S GIFT: BOOK ONE

JASMINE WALT

DYNAMO PRESS

ONE

"Have you thought a bit more about my marriage proposal, Dareena?"

Dareena gripped the broom handle a little tighter at the sound of Mr. Harrin's voice. Slowly, she turned to face her employer, who had managed to sneak up behind her while she swept, and carefully schooled her features to hide her instinctive wince.

Casler Harrin was a reedy man, about six feet tall, with thinning gray hair, mud-brown eyes, and a tobacco-stained beard. His lips were stretched into what Dareena imagined he thought was a smile, though really it was more of a leer, and she suppressed a shudder at the sight of his brown teeth. What would it be like to feel those thin lips pressed against hers? To feel those rough hands, already gnarling with age, push up her skirts within the privacy of their marriage bed?

"I haven't." Dareena turned her back to Mr. Harrin so she could sweep beneath one of the many tables. She'd taken advantage of the unexpected lull in customers to clean up a bit—with the sudden influx of people these past few days, there had barely been space enough to move about between the tables as she served drinks and took orders.

"And why the hell not?" Mr. Harrin's thick brows drew into a scowl.

She pulled a chair out of the way so she could get better access to the bits of food beneath the table. "Because you decided to ask two days before the Dragon's Hunt Festival, and we've had so many guests to take care of that I haven't had a chance to think about it."

Mr. Harrin gave a harsh laugh. "See, this is why I want you to be my wife," he chortled. He gave Dareena a hearty slap on her bottom before she could manage to get clear of him. "You're the only one with any sense around here, Dareena. The perfect person to take over the inn when I'm too old to work anymore."

Dareena held in a sigh. Truthfully, the prospect of inheriting the inn was a tempting one. As the daughter of a farmer who had passed away when she was only twelve, Dareena had little to look forward to. Mr. Harrin's offer was the most advantageous match she could hope for—it came with a fairly successful business, and when he died, she would be able to run it as she saw fit until their sons were of age to take it over.

Sons. An unwanted image of Mr. Harris leaning over her in bed, panting, popped into Dareena's head, and this time she *did* wince. Gods, could she really go through with it? The idea of sharing her bed with Mr. Harris was so repulsive—

"Dareena!" Tildy, one of the other serving girls, rushed in, her blue eyes sparkling. "The huntress has arrived!"

"Really?" Dareena's pulse jumped with excitement as all thoughts of marriage flew out of her head. "How do you know?"

"I just saw her ride in with her entourage," Tildy gushed. "She looks absolutely magnificent, with all that red hair and gleaming armor. I wish I could wear armor like that."

"Pah!" Mr. Harrin scoffed. "Armor is meant to be worn by men, not women. The only reason that huntress gets away with it is because of what she is."

Tildy frowned. "I never thought you would be one to speak ill of the dragons," she said. "The royal family is all that stands between us and the elves."

Mr. Harrin snorted. "The elves haven't attacked us for nearly a thousand years," he muttered, keeping his voice low, "and yet King Dragomir pushes us into this war as if they'd come in the middle of the night and slaughtered our babes. If he wants to harbor delusions, that's his business, but he doesn't need to keep raising my bloody taxes in the meantime."

He stomped off in a huff, leaving Tildy and Dareena to exchange uneasy looks. Dareena didn't know much about the War of the Three Kingdoms—the terrible battles fought between Dragonfell, Elvenhame, and Shadowhaven. And the only thing she knew about the current war was that it had started because King Dragomir believed the elves had killed his wife when she had dropped dead five years ago. But Dareena did know that what Mr. Harrin had said was tantamount to treason, and he was lucky the patrons in the corner were too drunk to pick up on it.

"Do you mind taking over for me for a bit?" Dareena asked. "I need to go see to Gilma."

"Of course," Tildy said. She fished a small cloth bag out of her apron pocket and handed it to Dareena. "My aunt had some cookies left over from today's batch—take them to her for me, will you?"

Dareena tucked the cookies into her skirt pocket and stepped out into the warm spring afternoon. The village was buzzing with activity—hammers clanged as craftsmen worked at their worktables and forges, vendors called in the distance as they pedaled their wares, and the smell of fresh-baked goods wafted up the street from the bakery Tildy's aunt owned.

Humming a cheery tune under her breath, Dareena navigated her way through the narrow streets toward Gilma's small house on the outskirts of town. On her way, she passed through the festival area, where tents had already been erected and vendors were setting up. Merchants of all kinds had traveled from the surrounding hamlets and villages to come to the Dragon's Hunt Festival in Hallowdale, and Dareena couldn't wait until festival day so she could walk through the streets and admire all the wares and performers.

Not that I will be able to afford much, she thought ruefully as a jeweler opened a glossy wooden case full of shiny silver rings. Mr. Harrin didn't pay her much since she mostly worked for room and board. Dareena's family had been stricken by consumption, and they'd all passed away when she was only twelve years old. For some reason, Dareena herself had never caught even a whiff of the illness that had taken her parents, but even so, she'd been unable to stay on the farm by herself. Women couldn't inherit property in Dragonfell unless it was gifted from their husband, so the farm would have passed to strangers anyway. Instead, Dareena had taken what she could and walked the twenty miles to Hallowdale. Mr. Harrin had been kind enough to take her in, and she'd been working for him for the past seven years.

And now he wanted to marry her.

Dareena truly wished she had better marriage prospects. Not that she didn't attract her fair share of attention—her lush figure, long raven hair, and emerald green eyes, which were a rare color amongst her people, turned quite a few heads. The way her skin remained smooth and pale despite being a working-class girl also worked in her favor. But the few men she'd taken a liking to had either been drafted in the war or had been persuaded by their parents to seek someone with better connections. Other than her looks and child-bearing hips, Dareena brought very little to the marriage table.

Mr. Harrin, on the other hand, would die within the next ten years or so. His arthritis pained him enough that it was hard to do simple tasks, and his eyesight had deteriorated to the point that Dareena was doing most of the accounting. She was thankful that her position had afforded her the opportunity to learn how to read and do numbers—many of the other village girls did not have either skill. The only reason he hadn't proposed to her before now was because, for the past ten years, all women had been forbidden to marry in view of the approaching Dragon's Hunt. Naturally, such restrictions caused consternation amongst the population, but it had been this way for centuries, and the last thing the kingdom needed was for the Dragon's Gift to accidentally marry someone other than the prince and start a family. But now that the hunt was approaching, families were beginning to make offers. Once the Dragon's Gift was found, which in the past had never taken more than a year, there would be a rash of weddings throughout the kingdom.

In the meantime, Mr. Harrin would demand that she pledge herself to him, and breaking a marriage pledge was a serious crime, payable by either a steep fine or up to a year in jail. Dareena had no intention of suffering either punishment—if she was to marry Mr. Harrin, she would have to do it soon after the Hunt.

Shuddering, she pushed the unpleasant thought out of her mind as she approached Gilma's ramshackle cottage. "Hello?" she called, rapping her knuckles on the faded green door.

"Dareena?" Gilma's thin voice answered. "You can come in."

Dareena eased open the door and stepped inside the dim interior. The musty smell that always accompanied the elderly, mixed with lavender, greeted Dareena as she closed the door behind her. Gilma was seated in a rocking chair by the hearth, her knitting needles in hand as she worked on a scarf. Her small, wrinkled face turned toward Dareena, her milky eyes unseeing. Dareena smiled at her even though she knew Gilma wouldn't be able to tell.

"How are you doing?" Dareena asked as she sat down on the stool next to the old woman. "Have you eaten today?"

"Haven't been hungry," she said. "But now that you're here, I could use a bite."

"Of course." Dareena rose from the chair and went to the small kitchen to fix a bowl of porridge. As she loaded some logs into the wood-burning stove, she thought, not for the first time, how lucky she was to still have her sight. Gilma's eyesight had already been weak when Dareena had first come to Hallowdale, but it had deteriorated rapidly over the past seven years. With no children alive to care for her, Dareena was the only person in the world she could rely on.

All the more reason for you to have children. You don't want to end up like this, alone and frail, with no one to care for you.

Dareena shook off the gloomy thought, then took a pot and filled it with water from the barrel that sat on the counter. There was no point in fretting about problems that had not yet come to pass.

"Are you looking forward to the Dragon's Hunt tomorrow?" Gilma asked.

"Oh yes," Dareena said, excitement filling her again. "I hear that there will be acrobats. There are so many people already here in town, we don't have rooms for them all." Indeed, many people had pitched tents in the fields outside the village.

"I wasn't even a twinkle in my father's eye during the last Dragon's Hunt," Gilma said sadly. "I had always thought I would be able to experience it with my own eyes, but instead I have to be shut up in this old house."

Dareena's stomach sank at Gilma's forlorn expression. She abandoned the pot on the stove and went to take the old woman's hand. "I promise I will tell you all about it when I return," she said. "I will give you so much detail, it will seem like you were there yourself!"

"If you return," Gilma pointed out. "There is always a possibility you might be Chosen."

"No, there isn't." Dareena laughed, patting Gilma's shoulder as she stood up again. "I'm the wrong color."

"Nonsense," Gilma protested. "The Dragon's Gift has been a blonde before."

Shaking her head, Dareena returned to the kitchen to check on the pot of water. She didn't bother to correct Gilma on her hair color—she would likely just forget anyway. Even though most of the residents from Hallowdale and the surrounding area had come out to enjoy the festivities and take advantage of the influx of full purses, the Dragon's Hunt had nothing to do with acrobats and merchants.

No, the Dragon's Hunt was exactly what it sounded like—a hunt. Every hundred years, the dragon king sent his daughters across Dragonfell to bring back three fertile women from each town. These women, the Chosen, were brought back to the Dragon's Keep, where they participated in a secret ritual that would identify if one of them was the Dragon's Gift—the sole woman in all of Dragonfell selected by the gods to be the next dragon king's mate.

Legend had it that long ago, during the War of the Three Kingdoms, the dragon king of the time did something to anger Shalia, Elvenhame's patron goddess. In retribution, the elven goddess rendered the female dragons of Dragonfell infertile with a terrible curse, with the intention of wiping out the entire dragon race.

Drogar, the dragon god, had been unable to undo Shalia's terrible curse, as the three gods were equally matched in strength. But out of sympathy for his people, he chose a human named Faria and imbued her with the ability to bear dragon sons and daughters. He presented her to the late dragon king's son and told him she was a gift and to treat her well, as another one of her kind would not be born for a hundred years.

And thus came about the Dragon's Hunt, a holy festival held every century to find the next Dragon's Gift.

Every woman dreamed of being selected by the huntresses to go to Dragon's Keep and participate in the sacred Selection Ritual, but Dareena had never held any illusions that she would ever see the inside of the Keep, much less become the Dragon's Gift. Throughout history, the Dragon's Gift had always been a flame-haired woman, with two exceptions, and those two had been endowed with golden tresses. Black-haired women like Dareena were never chosen, and in general were considered the least desirable. If not for Dareena's figure and startling eye color, she likely wouldn't attract male attention at all.

Of course, this year was a little different than most. For the previous nine hundred years, the Dragon's Gift had produced many daughters, but only one son. But the gods had smiled down on King Dragomir's late wife, for she had birthed not one, but three, dragon sons. They were all rumored to be exceedingly handsome and powerful, and because they were triplets, there was no guarantee as to which would inherit the throne.

"I suppose Lord Tirin's daughter will be amongst the Chosen," Gilma said, interrupting Dareena's musings. "Not that a selfish twat like that deserves to bear the next dragon king's sons."

"Gilma!" Dareena stifled a laugh as she stirred the pot of boiling oats.

"You know I'm right," Gilma said, completely unapologetic.

"Lyria Hallowdale may be dragon born, but she behaves no better than a harpy. The way she shrieks at even the tiniest slight, I'm surprised her father has any hearing left."

Dareena gave in to her laughter as she brought Gilma's porridge to a boil. "It's a good thing she's not around to hear you say that."

"Or what, she'll have me whipped?" Gilma scoffed. "Lyria might be cruel, but she's not stupid enough to do something like that. The whole town would be in an uproar if she whipped a poor old woman like me."

"True enough," Dareena said as she scooped up a spoonful of porridge and blew on it. The Hallowdales, just like every other noble family in Dragonfell, all had dragon's blood in them. They were either descended from dragon born or were dragon born themselves—offspring that came from the union of a dragon male and a human female. The dragon born could not shift or breathe fire like true dragons, but they were incredibly strong, impervious to most illnesses, and very intelligent.

Naturally, the Hallowdale family was inordinately proud of their dragon born ancestry, even though it came from an ancestor born nearly four hundred years ago. That didn't stop Lyria Hallowdale from strutting around and practically breathing fire on anyone who even remotely displeased her. But with her hourglass figure and flame-red curls, it was a given that she would be chosen by the huntress. It was only a matter of time.

Dareena fed Gilma her porridge, then cleaned up the kitchen and did a bit of tidying. "I've got to get back to the inn now," she told her. "Mr. Harrin will be needing my help with all these guests."

"Yes, I expect he will," Gilma said. "Before you go...I'd like you to do something for me."

"What is it?" Dareena asked, curious at the change in her tone.

"Go to the bedroom and fetch the dress all the way at the bottom of my clothing chest. You'll know the one—it's wrapped in a muslin cloth."

Frowning, Dareena did as Gilma asked. As she carefully rummaged through the clothing chest located at the foot of the bed, she wondered why Gilma wanted the dress. Did the old woman want to change into something more festive in honor of the Dragon's Hunt, even though she couldn't participate?

I suppose I can't blame her, she thought. *Even I want to dress up, and I barely have anything suitable.*

"Aha," Dareena said aloud as she pulled the muslin-wrapped package from the chest. She carefully put the rest of the clothes back, then went back into the other room.

"I found it," she said. "Do you want me to help you put it on?"

Gilma huffed. "Don't be silly, child. I could never wear something like this. Haven't you opened it yet?"

"I..." Flustered, Dareena put the package on the stool, then delicately unwrapped it. She gasped as she held up the dress—a gorgeous deep red linen with long sleeves and a high waistline. The scoop neckline and waist were embroidered in shimmering gold thread, and the skirt hung to the floor.

"My daughter wore that dress on her wedding day," Gilma

said, smiling sadly. "I've held onto it all these years as a keepsake, but it's time to put it to good use again."

"Oh, no." Dareena held out the dress to Gilma before she remembered she couldn't see it. "I couldn't possibly—"

"Wear it to the festival tomorrow, and make me proud, Dareena," Gilma said before Dareena could protest further. "If any dress will help you catch the eye of the huntress, it's this one."

Tears sprang to Dareena's eyes, and she swallowed against a sudden lump in her throat. "I will," she promised, gathering the dress to her chest. There was no chance of Dareena being chosen as the Dragon's Gift, but this dress was fit for a noble lady—something Lyria herself might wear.

For just one day, Dareena could forget that she was lowborn, and about Mr. Harris's marriage proposal. She could put on that dress and glide through the festival with her head held high while pretending she was a lady, not the daughter of a no-name farmer. It was a once-in-a-lifetime chance, and she damn well wasn't going to squander it.

TWO

"Alistair," Drystan said, trying not to be too annoyed as his brother paced restlessly on the red and gold carpet in his office. "Would you mind telling me exactly why you're wearing a hole in my carpet?"

"It's not technically your office," Alistair pointed out, though he did stop pacing. "And I didn't realize you cared more about furniture than you did your favorite brother."

Drystan frowned. Though this office wasn't officially assigned to anyone, Drystan considered it his—he came here when he needed to concentrate, mainly because it was far enough from their father's apartments that he wouldn't usually be disturbed. No such luck today, though. His brother had hunted him down, determined to enunciate everything already weighing heavily on his mind.

"That may all be true," Drystan said, "but you're still bothering me. Would you just tell me what's on your mind, so I can tell you everything will be all right and then kick you out of here so I can concentrate?"

Alistair laughed. "The same thing that's on all of our minds, brother. The Hunt."

Drystan let out a long sigh. Today marked the beginning of the Dragon's Hunt—the first one of the year. Drystan and his brothers were all too aware of how unlikely they were to be successful in their quest the first time around. Some generations had to live through half a dozen Hunts before they found their Dragon's Gift.

But that wasn't why the brothers had been tense since the moment the huntresses had been dispatched to all ten provinces of Dragonfell to pick out the most beautiful women in the land. No, they were tense because they faced a problem no dragon prince had since the War of the Three Kingdoms had ended and the dragons had been stricken by Shalia's Curse.

The problem of succession.

Drystan got along with his two brothers; he was fiercely protective of both and knew without a doubt that either would take an arrow through the heart to save him. He felt no animosity toward them, and it had never been their way to fight over anything, especially a woman.

But this was different. The Dragon's Gift could only wed one man, and for the past thousand years, there had only been one prince for her to wed. This time, there were three—Drystan, Lucyan, and Alistair. And because they were triplets, it was not entirely clear who would be named their father's heir.

From a young age, the brothers had been told that it would be down to King Dragomir, their father, to choose a son to succeed him. And the choice would come down to which brother was best suited to rule.

Drystan, of course, thought he was that man—aside from being the eldest, he was also the most responsible and had the most experience in leadership positions. Lucyan was just too mischievous, always scheming, and while that particular quality made him a powerful ally, kings weren't supposed to be quite as devious. Alistair, on the other hand, was the soldier with the heart of gold—good on the battlefield, but when his armor was off, he was far too gentle and idealistic.

"I doubt Father will pick Lucyan," Alistair reasoned. "I mean, who in their right mind would give a kingdom to Lucyan?"

"In their *right mind*," Drystan emphasized, because therein lay a substantial issue. Their father wasn't exactly sane. Once, Drystan had looked upon his father as a god—a man who could do no wrong, who ruled with a wise and steady hand. He had taught them how to ride, had play-wrestled with them in the fields, and had delighted them with his mastery of fire manipulation.

But as the brothers had grown into adults, they'd watched their father become more bloodthirsty, impulsive, and even cruel.

The change had been subtle at first—shortness of temper, less willing to listen to his council and his sons. But the affliction had rapidly escalated after their mother died five years ago. He had grown capricious, making impulsive decisions despite the clear advice from his council, and he was downright nasty to petitioners to the point that hardly anyone in the kingdom would dare approach him anymore, even his vassals.

No one would speak of it openly, but the whispers at court made it clear—everyone knew the king was being taken by madness.

Hence why, while they couldn't count on it, everyone hoped that this Hunt would be successful. If they found the Dragon's Gift this week, the king would name a successor and ensure that Dragonfell was still standing when the day of his demise came.

Of course, there was still the issue of figuring out how to prevent the king from bringing about the entire kingdom's demise before he passed away. But Drystan knew better than to focus on more than one problem at a time—

"Right, right. But let's presume that, for once, our father is led by reason. Lucyan is a no. He sees life itself as a game of kings and queens."

Drystan nodded, although he didn't quite agree. True, Lucyan was a master puppeteer, but what Alistair failed to acknowledge was that their middle brother excelled at it.

"Me," Alistair pondered out loud. "I'm..."

"Gullible? Easy to manipulate? No, I know. Badly dressed."

Alistair lifted a brow at that one. He was as casual as Drystan liked to be reserved, in leather pants and a loose shirt, while Drystan was in a well-cut formal gray tunic embellished only by a bit of silver thread. Either of them need only throw their reinforced armor on top to be ready for battle at a moment's notice, as was necessary in times of war, but their style couldn't have been more different.

"And yet, all the ladies prefer me, don't they?"

Drystan smirked. Let him believe that, if it pleased him. He wouldn't crush his delusions.

"Not to mention," Alistair continued, "that you desperately need to remove the broomstick that has been firmly lodged in your ass since puberty if you're to win over the lady, whoever she might be."

That made him laugh. "Right. I'm sure Father will take into consideration who amongst us has her favor."

The very thought was ludicrous. Nothing mattered less to the king. He only cared about which of the brothers was most likely to sire the strongest dragons.

"Come on, then, hazard a guess. Who amongst us will our father choose?"

"He most probably won't have to choose anyone, brother. At least not yet. The odds of the Dragon's Gift being found our first time are slim."

"But you must wonder."

Drystan sighed. "Father isn't by any means predictable. My guess is he'll surprise us."

It wasn't an answer, because how was he supposed to say, *I believe he'll choose me?*

Alistair was about to argue again, determined to heckle Drystan as much as possible, when an arrow flew through the open window. Both princes lunged into action, swords drawn, their chests filling with fire as they looked out the window.

The city didn't seem disrupted, and no guard had been alerted. Drystan's gaze went beyond their walls, to the dark and dangerous forest where no one went unaccompanied. No one could have shot through such a small opening at that distance.

No one but an elf.

"Shit." Alistair dislodged the arrow from the wall while Drystan's attention stayed fixed on the trees. Rage burned hot in his chest, and he wrestled with his temper for several long seconds. Finally, he managed to speak.

"Call the Guard."

"That may not be wise, brother."

He turned to Alistair, incredulous. His brother held a long, curved piece of parchment. So, they'd sent a threat, had they? He'd respond in kind.

"You'll want to read this."

"They'll say nothing I wish to hear."

The war between the elves of Elvenhame and the dragons of Dragonfell had started when the long-eared scum had murdered their mother, their father's mate and Dragon's Gift. They hadn't gone after the powerful king, or even after them— no, they'd killed a defenseless woman with no more skill than humans aside from her ability to birth dragons. No crime was more hideous and cowardly. The only thing he wanted of elves was to hear their screams as he burned them to ashes.

"Calm yourself, Drystan. This is about Taldren."

That got his attention.

Taldren was family—their cousin, to be exact. While only the children of the king and his Dragon's Gift were born as dragons, they had distant relatives who were descended from the dragons that had existed before Shalia's Curse had been inflicted upon them. While the female dragons of that time had been unable to bear children, the males had not been rendered infertile. To ensure their lines didn't die out completely, they bedded human women, creating a hybrid race known as the dragon born. The dragon born of old had been able to breathe fire and were immortal, though they could not shift themselves. The ones today were a watered-down version—fire-resistant, fast healers, and though they lived longer than humans, it was only by a few decades.

Even so, all dragon born were considered descendants of the royal family, and Taldren in particular was descended from one of King Rakan's nephews. He might be their cousin ten times removed, but Taldren was still family, and they'd grown up sparring and playing together.

"Blast it," Alistair growled. "He should have never been sent to the front."

"They'll want to use him as leverage," Drystan guessed. Quite devious of the elves, using their friend to get to them, but they wouldn't fall for it. They couldn't afford to. Taldren understood the rules of war, and he'd die knowing he'd be avenged. That was all they could offer him.

"I can almost read you, brother. You're thinking about doing right by the kingdom and letting your oldest friend rot."

"And you're thinking about carelessly risking yourself and jumping to the rescue."

Hence why Drystan would be king.

"Actually, no," Alistair replied, rolling the parchment and putting it in his pocket. "I'm thinking we should pay a visit to the most conniving one of us."

Lucyan lived close to the king's apartment, where he heard every rumor before anyone else. He preferred making people come to him, rather than the other way around, which Drystan couldn't blame him for. Holding conversations or negotiations on your turf nearly always gave you the upper hand.

Anyone else might have knocked, but Drystan bypassed the formality. He shouldered his brother's door wide open, preparing to storm inside and deliver the dire news.

And regretted it immediately.

Despite the fact that it was just after noon, and although he hadn't seen it necessary to lock his door, their brother was, for lack of a better term, fucking a lady's mouth. A married lady, too, if he recognized the long blonde hair, the perky nose, and the beauty spot just below her eye.

"Really?" Alistair asked, peering over Drystan's shoulder. "Laureline Destrange?" The poor gal hadn't had a ring on her finger for more than a month, and already he'd managed to add her name to the long list of mistresses who'd serviced him.

Lucyan turned toward them with a sigh. "We're going to have to finish this early, love. It appears that my dearest brothers have gotten themselves into another mess."

Drystan wanted to argue that they could have visited him for any reason, but he didn't bother. Lucyan had a point—they never came to his place unless they had to, precisely because scenes like this were all too common. Call him mad, but Drystan didn't quite feel like talking while his brother's trousers were around his ankles.

Drystan couldn't decide which one of his brothers was the most hopeless in matters of the fairer sex: Alistair, who'd ended up with so many gold diggers, or Lucyan, who had a new mistress every half day. But then again, the last two women Drystan had taken to his bed hadn't been gems either. It was fortunate that their father had every intention of picking their breeders when the time came. Better to let a madman choose than to leave them to their own devices, at least in this matter.

"Come on," he growled to Alistair, turning around and nudging his brother back into the hall. "Let's give Lucyan time to pull his britches up."

Luckily, Lucyan didn't keep them waiting too long. Five minutes later, Mrs. Destrange sailed out of the room looking oddly satisfied for a woman who hadn't even climaxed. She gave a smile and a wink to Lucyan, who grinned back as he waved his brothers in.

"Oh, quit looking at me like that," Lucyan said as he closed the door behind them. "Her husband is quite aware of this arrangement. He owed me a favor and chose to pay it that way. Who am I to say nay?"

"Who indeed?" Alistair smirked. "You've never been able to say no to pussy in your life, Lucyan. I imagine that if an elven princess showed up outside your door buck naked, you'd gladly fuck her before chaining her up in the dungeons."

"Or perhaps *while* chaining her up in the dungeons." He waggled his eyebrows, and Drystan buried a sigh. Lucyan was always trying to get a rise out of him. "Anyway, enough of the small talk. Tell me what Alistair has done this time."

Alistair scowled. "How do you know I did anything?"

"Because nine times out of ten, you're the one in hot water."

"Actually," Drystan said, interrupting his brothers before

things could devolve further, "it has nothing to do with Alistair. We've received a missive from Elvenhame."

Lucyan shed his pleasant humor, his face becoming a cold mask. "Show me the letter," he commanded.

Drystan wordlessly handed over the scroll. Lucyan scanned it twice, his amber eyes hard, then turned it around and checked the seal before sniffing the paper. Finally, he rolled it up and tucked it into his vest.

"You're not to speak of this to anyone else," Lucyan said firmly when Drystan opened his mouth to protest. "I'll alert the right guards and make them ambush these lowlifes at the rendezvous point they've set."

"They clearly state that we should come, and come alone, if we're to see Taldren alive again."

"Taldren is probably already dead," Lucyan growled. "They just want a chance at one, if not three, of the heirs of Dragonfell, and we *won't* give them one." He was usually the most controlled amongst them, yet his eyes blazed red rather than their regular amber. Alistair started to speak, but Drystan shook his head. He knew this look. He knew exactly what their brother was up to. Arguing right now was pointless.

"You came to me because you knew I'd know best. Will you leave this matter in my hands?" Lucyan asked, his voice quiet.

"Very well," Drystan said.

"Alistair?" Lucyan looked pointedly at their youngest brother.

Alistair grumbled, but relented. "Fine. But Taldren had better come out of this alive. I don't care what you say—he's not dead yet."

He stalked out of the room, and Drystan followed. As soon as they were out of earshot, Alistair rounded on him, incredulous. "Just leave it up to the guards? I didn't expect that from Lucyan. Not at all."

"Of course not. Our brother isn't one to abandon the fate of a friend to strangers. And he won't."

Alistair paused. "He plans to go by himself?"

Drystan smiled. This was what most people completely missed when they thought of cruel, unfeeling Lucyan. Yes, he saw no issue sacrificing a pawn to get what he wanted. But given the right motivation, he would use the most relevant piece in his elaborate game: himself. It wasn't the first time he'd selflessly put himself forward rather than endangering one of his brothers.

"Think about it. The elves want three princes, and if they succeed in capturing or killing us, our entire kingdom is doomed. If only one turns up…"

Alistair shook his head, torn between amusement and exasperation. "Of course. I should have seen it."

"It's a good thing you've got me around, then." Drystan clapped him on the shoulder, then turned him about. "Now, shall we go before him or follow him at a distance?"

THREE

"**A**nd just where do you think you're going in a dress like that?"

Dareena froze halfway to the door at the sound of Mr. Harrin's voice. Turning, she saw him standing farther down the hall, eyes glittering, arms folded across his chest. He looked her up and down in a way that sent unpleasant shivers down her spine—his gaze was lascivious and displeased all at once.

"To the festival, of course," Dareena said calmly. "All women of age are required to attend and are automatically given the day off by order of the king. You know that."

Mr. Harrin grunted. "Idiotic rule, that," he said. "Taking away my most valuable employee on the busiest day of the century. You're not going to get picked, anyway."

"I know that," Dareena said, "but even so, I am required to attend." She didn't bother telling him that she was actually looking forward to the festival. That would only make him grumpier.

"If you know that, then why did you bother putting on such a fancy dress?" Mr. Harrin's eyes narrowed. "Where did you get that thing, anyway? You can't afford to buy something as fancy as that."

"It was a gift from Gilma," Dareena said evenly, even as her anxiety rose. Would Mr. Harrin actually try to prevent her from leaving? Legally, he couldn't, and the moment someone saw her waiting tables, the guards would be called to drag her away. But he could always throw her into the cellar, if he had a mind to. Even though he was an old man, he was still stronger than her.

"Then wear it to our wedding," Mr. Harrin insisted. "Come on, Dareena, you don't need to waste your time on a sham like this." He grabbed Dareena's arm as she turned to leave. "You're not going to be Chosen. Your best bet is to pledge yourself to me."

"And so what if it is a sham?" Dareena protested, trying to yank her arm from his strong grip. "I deserve at least *one* good day off. I'm not going to pass up this opportunity to have a good time just because you're worried about something that won't come to pass. Let me go, Mr. Harrin."

"Fine," he huffed, releasing her. "But don't get too friendly with any of the men. We've got a wedding to plan, Dareena."

Dareena left as quickly as she could without actually running. She didn't correct Mr. Harrin on his assumption—there was always a chance that she *would* accept his marriage proposal, and if she rejected him now he might very well set his sights elsewhere.

Stop that, she scolded herself as her heart began to sink toward her shoes. It was a lovely day, with music and laughter ringing in the air, and the smell of sugary pastries and roasting meat. She would not let Mr. Harrin spoil this special day for her.

"Dareena!" Tildy squealed, distracting Dareena from her melancholy. She turned to see Tildy running up the street toward her, bedecked in a sunny yellow dress she'd worked on all year. "By the dragon, where did you get that dress? It's stunning!"

"Gilma gave it to me," Dareena said, sweeping Tildy into a hug. "But yours looks far lovelier. It looks even better on you than I thought it would!"

Beaming, Tildy performed a quick little spin to show off the dress. As she did, a trio of men walking past paused to look. Tildy might not have had the choicest figure, but she had rosy cheeks and flaxen hair and looked like a ray of sunshine in the middle of the street.

"Come on," she said, grabbing Dareena's hand. "Let's go to the festival!"

The two women raced down the street together, holding hands and laughing like they were little children again. Soon, they found themselves amidst the sea of tents Dareena had walked through yesterday, but this time they were all set up and boasting all manner of goods and entertainments. To their left, a soothsayer read fortunes from people's palms. To their right, a merchant from farther south was selling brilliantly colored handwoven rugs. Farther up the path, a man in brightly colored clothing lay on a mat, contorting himself into all kinds of impossible positions as the small crowd gasped in horror and amazement.

"There is truly something here for everyone," Dareena murmured.

Tildy and Dareena spent the rest of the morning wandering through the tents, sampling the food and marveling over the wares. Dareena attracted a good deal of attention—quite a few women asked her how she came by the dress and where they could get one for themselves. Several men asked Dareena to dance, and before she knew it, she was swept off to the dancing square along with Tildy.

The dancing square had been set up in the center of the festival area, with various performers playing lively, upbeat tunes that got the blood pumping and Dareena's feet moving almost of their own accord. She quickly found herself separated from Tildy as she danced with partner after partner, until nearly two hours later, she finally begged off for a drink, sweaty and more than a little flushed from all the dancing.

"Well, you look like you've been having a jolly good time," the woman behind the lemonade stand chuckled as Dareena ordered a dipperful. She groaned as the cool, sweet liquid hit her tongue—lemonade was a rare treat, and it was easily one of the best things she'd tasted in a long time.

"I've been dancing for the last two hours," she said breathlessly, wiping her mouth with the back of her hand. "I think I'll be needing another one of those—I'm parched!"

She paid for another drink, and then, feeling refreshed, wandered through the tents for a while on her own. Tildy would catch up to her eventually, and after all that dancing, she felt like being by herself for a bit.

None of the men she'd danced with had dared to follow her when she'd left—it was perfectly acceptable to ask the women to dance, but trying to lay claim to any of them before the Hunt had finished was forbidden. The dragon king would be extremely displeased if one of the Chosen had lain with a man on the day of the festival—if the Dragon's Gift came to the castle already pregnant, it would be an absolute disaster.

Still, Dareena thought as her mind wandered back to the last man she'd danced with. His name was Cole Barris, he was the son of Hallowdale's treasurer, and he had seemed awfully interested. Why shouldn't Dareena invite him to dance with her again? He would be a good match, much more pleasing to the eye than Mr. Harrin, and well-off enough that she would be taken care of. It wasn't as if Dareena would actually be Chosen —everyone knew that with her coloring, it was impossible.

"You bitch!" a familiar voice shrieked, cutting through the gay atmosphere. "You've ruined my outfit!"

Dareena spun around to see Lyria standing a few feet away in front of a vendor cart selling pieces of honeycomb. Honey had dribbled down the front of her dress, staining her white bodice, as she clutched a piece of honeycomb that had undoubtedly just been handed to her. The vendor, a slim, mousy-looking girl, trembled, her brown eyes wide with fear.

"I'm sorry, miss, but I did warn you—"

"You did no such thing!" Lyria's cheeks were pink with rage. "You simply handed it to me like the thoughtless twit you are, with no regard for my outfit. Do you have any idea how much this dress cost? More than what your silly cart makes in a year, I'd wager!"

She lifted her hand to slap the girl, but before the blow could connect, Dareena stepped in.

"You should be more careful," she said, grabbing Lyria's hand. "You never know where your hand might land if you keep swinging it about like that."

"Dareena," Lyria spat, her blue eyes sparking with anger. She yanked her hand from Dareena's grip. "Get out of my way. This insolent whore needs to be punished!"

"Do you really want to be seen smacking around a helpless girl on the day of the Dragon's Hunt?" Dareena asked, arching an eyebrow. "The huntress and her escorts are everywhere. They could be watching you right now."

"Don't be ridiculous," Lyria said, but her eyes darted around, looking to see if the huntress was, in fact, watching. "The huntress wouldn't care. I'm sure she punishes impudent servants all the time. It comes with the territory of being royalty," she added with a smirk.

Dareena stared at her for a long moment. "I would change that dress, if I were you," she said. "White really isn't your color."

Lyria gasped, and Dareena marched away before the woman could answer. She half expected Lyria to yank her back by the hair, but she must have taken her warning about the huntress watching to heart, because nothing happened.

It took a few minutes for Dareena to cool off after the encounter. Eventually, she slowed her pace, then stopped at an apple cart. As she munched on a golden apple, she reflected that the one good thing about Lyria being Chosen was that at least Hallowdale would be rid of her for a few weeks. But it had been foolish of Dareena to slight her that way, especially in such a public fashion. If Lyria didn't become the next Dragon's Gift, she would make Dareena's life hell when she returned to Hallowdale.

"Well, hello there," a female voice purred in her ear, cutting off her train of thought. "You're a pretty one, aren't you?"

Slowly, Dareena turned toward the voice. Her heart stopped at the sight of a tall, flame-haired woman leaning against one of the tent poles behind her, dressed in shining armor. The dragon crest emblazoned on her chest left no doubt in Dareena's mind as to who she was.

"Huntress," she murmured, dipping into a deep curtsy. How long had the huntress been standing there? And why did she want to speak to Dareena, of all people?

"Rise," the woman said, a curious note in her voice. "What is your name? I don't recall you amongst any of the noble families I met with yesterday."

Dareena's face flushed as she realized the woman's mistake. "My name is Dareena Sellis. I am a serving girl at the Hallowdale Inn."

"A serving girl?" The huntress blinked in surprise. "You don't look it in that dress. Where did you steal that?"

Dareena stiffened at the insult. "I didn't steal it from anyone," she said coldly, raising her chin to meet the huntress's gaze squarely. The huntress's eyes narrowed, and Dareena forced herself not to flinch.

What in blue blazes are you doing? a voice—likely the voice of reason—screamed in Dareena's mind. *You should throw your-self on the ground and beg her forgiveness before she burns you to a crisp!*

But to Dareena's surprise, the woman threw back her head and laughed. "You have fire," she said. "You will do."

"W-what?" Dareena sputtered as the huntress started to move past. "Do for what?"

The huntress paused. "You seem like a woman who is prone to speak her mind," she said, turning around. "What do you think of Lyria, the lord's daughter?"

"She's very beautiful," Dareena said cautiously. "But I'm afraid that her particular beauty only runs skin-deep." Had the huntress witnessed her altercation with Lyria after all?

Dareena expected the huntress to be disappointed or displeased, but to her surprise, the woman grinned. "I think we're going to get along just fine," she said, and with that parting remark, disappeared into the crowd.

"Did she really say that?" Tildy asked, astonished. The two women sat in the grass, feasting on a pair of turkey legs for dinner. The high noon sun shone on them, turning Tildy's hair to gold and illuminating the sparkle in her eyes.

"She did," Dareena said. "But I have no idea what she could mean. Do you think she wants me as a handmaiden?" The thought worried her. She had absolutely no training or experience in that kind of work, and she wasn't particularly keen on spending her days around royalty. That said, it might still beat the prospect of lying with Mr. Harrin every night.

Tildy snorted. "A woman like that would want a squire, not a handmaiden," she said. "It really sounds like she's thinking about picking you."

Dareena shook her head. "We already know who's going to get picked," she said around a mouthful of meat. "Lyria is the top choice, and I'm betting Cyra will be right behind her."

"If anyone deserves to be queen, it's Cyra," Tildy said, an admiring look in her eye. Cyra was the daughter of a wealthy merchant, and she spent much of her spare time looking after the homeless. "She would rule with a gentle hand."

"The Dragon's Gift doesn't actually have any authority," Dareena reminded her. "She is only there to bear the king's children. Beyond that, she isn't given any responsibilities."

Tildy huffed. "I think that's ridiculous. If the gods consider a woman worthy enough to be the Dragon's Gift, then surely they consider her worthy of greater responsibility. Women should have a say when it comes to how this country is run."

Dareena smiled. "Perhaps one day things will change," she said, though she doubted it. The kingdom of Dragonfell only recognized power, and women had none. That was why the only females in the Dragon Force were the king's daughters and the odd dragon born female. Everyone else who wielded either weapons or the power of office was male.

"Well, there's no point in worrying about things we can't change," Tildy said, tossing her bone aside. "Let's enjoy the festival while it lasts."

The two women spent the rest of the afternoon doing just that—talking and laughing with friends, enjoying spectacles from various performers, and simply relishing the rarity of a day off. Most of the townsfolk, with the exception of nobles, were forced to toil day in and day out to scrape a living. It was nice to be able to take some time off and simply appreciate friends and family and the joy of being alive, even if it was just for this one day.

But soon enough, dusk descended upon Hallowdale, and with it, quiet. Everyone knew that the time was growing near, and the air grew charged with anticipation.

Finally, the quiet was broken by the signal they'd all been waiting for—the drums. A single beat echoed through the tents, over and over, calling everyone away from the festival and to the town square. Guards herded all of the marriageable women together, pushing through the crowds. Tildy and Dareena grabbed hands to keep from being separated.

"I'm nervous," Tildy whispered as they were lined up in two rows facing each other. "I didn't expect to be nervous."

"I know what you mean," Dareena whispered back, looking up to the podium. Lord Hallowdale stood there, and behind him, the huntress who had come down from Dragon's Keep to choose the three women who would participate in the Selection Ritual. Two soldiers flanked her, and they all looked magnificent and foreboding, the waning sunlight setting their armor and hair ablaze, their expressions somehow fierce and stoic at once. Standing before them was enough to make anyone nervous, and as Dareena glanced around, she saw that she and Tildy weren't the only ones.

In fact, the only one who didn't seem nervous was Lyria

Hallowdale. She stood tall and proud at the front of the line opposite Dareena, in an ivory gown rather than the white she'd worn earlier. Dareena bristled at the faintest hint of smugness on Lyria's aristocratic features. She was obviously counting her chickens already.

And why shouldn't she? Dareena asked herself. If she were in Lyria's position, she would be just as confident.

"Citizens of Hallowdale," Lord Hallowdale boomed as the drums finally silenced. He looked quite regal dressed in a red and gold tunic likely worth a lifetime of Dareena's wages. "We are gathered here today to celebrate one of the holiest events in our country's history—the Dragon's Hunt."

The whole town listened as Lord Hallowdale launched into a lengthy explanation of the history of the Dragon's Hunt. It was nothing Dareena hadn't heard before, so she listened with only half an ear, her attention on the women standing behind him. The huntress she had met was there, but Dareena had not met the two female soldiers flanking her. There was something similar about their features, as if they might be distantly related, but the huntress was the only one with the amber eyes that all dragons bore. They all wore the armor of the Dragon Force, though, and since only dragon-blooded females were allowed in the Dragon Force, the other two must be dragon born.

Finally, Lord Hallowdale finished his monologue. "We are honored by the presence of General Tariana, who has been sent by King Dragomir to conduct the Hunt on his behalf." He gestured to the amber-eyed huntress, and Dareena struggled to keep her jaw from dropping. Tariana was the *general* of Dragonfell's Dragon Force? "She and her entourage have watched the women of our fair city throughout the day and will now begin the ceremonial walk before announcing the Chosen."

The three women descended from the podium, and every woman on the ground stood a little taller. They slowly prowled down the center of the two lines together, meeting the gaze of each woman they passed. Some of the women flinched, while others held themselves ramrod stiff beneath their regard.

Relax, Dareena told herself. She forced her muscles to loosen, and as she did, some of the nerves began to ease. This was nothing to be afraid of. The huntress would finish her walk, announce the Chosen, and then Dareena would go home. She would hold onto the memory of this extraordinary day as she went back to her ordinary life, and that would be that.

By the time the huntress and her entourage came to where Dareena and Tildy stood, Dareena was calm and collected. She met the first dragon born's eyes without flinching and was utterly unsurprised when the woman's gaze flicked away quickly. The other dragon born's assessment was the same, and Tariana didn't even look at her. Dareena couldn't help but feel a little disappointed—after their talk earlier, she'd thought the huntress would at least acknowledge her.

But then again, perhaps it was for the best that she didn't. There was no point in getting her hopes up that perhaps the huntress had seen something in Dareena that the others did not. Dareena *herself* didn't see anything within that would help her stand out, so why should anybody else?

Eventually, after what seemed like an age, the huntress and her entourage returned to the stage. The three women bowed their heads, whispering together. A minute passed, and then the entire world seemed to go silent as Tariana stepped forward, pulling a small scroll from her sleeve.

"They must have made their decision beforehand," Tildy whispered, and Dareena gave the barest of nods. Of course they had—that's why they'd spent the day watching the women.

"After some deliberation," Tariana said, her voice echoing loud and clear, "we have made our decision. Will the following women please come forth."

The crowd held their breath as Tariana slowly opened the scroll. "Cyra Lannen, come forth."

The crowd erupted into cheers as Cyra stepped from the ranks, a smile beaming from her lovely face. She moved confidently to the podium, then dipped into a deep curtsy.

"Mira Fallen, come forth," Tariana called next, and Dareena blinked in surprise. Dareena had expected Lyria to be called first, but since Cyra was so popular, it hadn't been strange that the huntress had chosen to call her first instead. But to have Mira called next...she was a beauty, with strawberry-blonde hair and pretty, almost elfin features, but she was lowborn. The brief flash of annoyance on Lyria's face confirmed she had not missed the slight, and Dareena wondered if Tariana had something against her. She had not seemed surprised at Dareena's not-so-subtle hint that Lyria was rotten.

Mira practically sprang out of line before she remembered herself, her whole body vibrating with excitement as the towns-folk clapped and cheered. Dareena hid a smile as Mira visibly forced herself to approach at a sedate pace, then curtsied awkwardly to the huntress before taking her place next to Cyra.

"And now, for our final selection..." Tariana paused, her

gaze going to Lyria. Dareena's heart sank. She had just begun to hope that the huntress might have passed over Lyria for someone worthier, but it was not to be. The crowd went silent, waiting for the inevitable.

But then Tariana's lips curved into a wicked smile, and those amber eyes snapped to Dareena's. "Dareena Sellis," the general said, and Dareena's world seemed to slide out from beneath her feet. "Come forth."

FOUR

After Lucyan's brothers left, he spent the day quite leisurely, or so it appeared. He lounged around in his quarters for another hour, then saddled his horse and informed the captain of the guard that he was going into town for a bit.

Paxhall was the capital of Dragonfell and home of Dragon's Keep. It housed several hundred thousand inhabitants and was easily one of the largest cities in Terragaard. Only Inkwall, Shadowhaven's capital, was larger—the city was home to all sort of black magic and trickery, or so Lucyan had been brought up to believe. In reality, it was a bustling city, as Lucyan had discovered the one time he'd managed to slip in and visit the place. Inkwall was filled with as much good and evil as anywhere else.

In fact, aside from its burgeoning population of magic users, Inkwall wasn't very different from Paxhall. Both towns were filled with merchants and bookshops and brothels and wineries, and both had their share of nobles and vagrants. The man

Lucyan sought today was somewhere in the middle—a trader who kept a booth down at merchants' square and dealt in exotic collectibles from all over the world.

"How do you do, Sidren?" Lucyan asked as he stopped in front of the trader's stall.

Sidren was a tall, rotund man with a shiny bald head and a thick mustache. He wore a broad smile as he finished a transaction with a hooded young man, but that smile faded as he turned to Lucyan.

"My prince!" Sidren's nut-brown skin blanched at the sight of Lucyan. "I...I did not realize you would call again so soon."

Lucyan hid a smile. "Relax, Sidren. I'm not here to give you any grief." He honestly didn't know why the trader continued to get jittery whenever Lucyan dropped by—he'd already made it clear that he'd forgiven him for his offense. Selling to elves— particularly magical objects that could be used to fight against them during the war—was treason, and therefore punishable by death. Someone more shortsighted, like Drystan, or perhaps even Alistair, would have sent Sidren to meet his fate, but not Lucyan.

Sidren's stall was known for one very valuable thing: it often had magical scrolls, potions, and amulets hidden beneath the fancy furs and trinkets brought back from his regular dealings with the warlocks. Much of what he sold were watered down versions of real magic, which was why Lucyan didn't pay him much mind. But every once in a while, Sidren brought home the real thing.

"Oh. All right then." Sidren visibly relaxed. "What can I do for you, my friend?"

My friend. Lucyan often used the term himself when negotiating—not because the person in question was *really* his friend, but it was always a good idea to make the people you used feel important.

Lucyan leaned in and lowered his voice. "I'm hoping you might have an object that can help me get in and out of the palace without being seen."

Sidren pursed his lips. "That is powerful magic, my prince. Not very many have the power to turn invisible."

Lucyan cocked his head. "Is that a no?"

"I would never refuse you, my prince, if I was able to..." He trailed off, his eyes widening as inspiration struck. "Hang on," he muttered, ducking beneath the table to rummage through one of his many trunks. "I may have just the thing."

He emerged a few moments later with a ratty old cloak that smelled strongly of damp.

"What is this?" Lucyan asked as he gingerly took it from the trader.

"You'll excuse its state, my prince," Sidren said, a little anxiously. "It isn't for sale, and I've had no use for it in years. This is an invisibility cloak. Normally I wouldn't think to part with it, but the magic is beginning to fail. It can only be used for an hour a day."

"An hour a day?" Lucyan frowned. "If it's failing, how do I know the spell will truly last an hour? What if it dies after a few minutes and leaves me exposed?"

Sidren shrugged. "That's the risk you'll have to take if you want to use it, my prince. It also won't muffle noises or prevent someone from detecting you with magic."

"Lovely," Lucyan muttered, holding the cloak up to the light for inspection. Thankfully, the fabric had no holes in it—the last thing he needed was for one of his body parts to be floating, disembodied, while he was trying to be stealthy. "Would cleaning it affect the magic?"

"I'm not sure," Sidren admitted. "I've never risked it."

Lucyan rolled his eyes. *That* was obvious. "If the smell alerts the guards, this won't be much help." But it wasn't the guards Lucyan was wary of, so he relented. "Fine, I'll take it. How much do I owe you?"

"For you, my prince? Nothing."

Ah. Lucyan smiled—the man was smarter than he thought. "Until next time, then," he said, and took his leave. Sidren had just earned a favor, and everyone knew that a favor from Lucyan was worth far more than a piece of gold.

LUCYAN NEEDED TO ACT PROMPTLY, and more importantly, without being hindered by his well-meaning, yet terribly incompetent, brothers. They suspected he was up to something, of course. He always was. No matter, though; if they couldn't see him leave, they wouldn't be able to interfere, and that was all he needed.

The stakes were too high this time. It wasn't simply about rescuing their friend; Lucyan wasn't that shortsighted. If it had just been for Taldren's benefit, he wouldn't have seen the need to cut his brothers off.

Lucyan took the letter out of his back pocket and looked at

its seal again. There it was, that clear signature under the shape of an elven tree: Andur, the High King.

If there was even a small chance that the king of elves was really behind this, it meant he would send high elves, noble borns of Elvenhame. Elves who would know which one of them had murdered his mother.

Lucyan would extract the truth from their dying breaths.

Adorned by his newly obtained invisibility cloak, Lucyan had no issues leaving the Keep. He followed a dozen guards out, their metallic armor making enough racket to tune out the sound of his agile steps. He had to travel light, but it didn't matter. He might not be able to shift yet, but he could still breathe fire and move with superhuman speed. A short sword and two knives stuck in his boots were more than enough to suit his purpose.

The guards turned left at the gate, heading toward their western borders, and Lucyan made his way to the forest. He shed the cloak once he'd reached the dark, uninviting woods and continued on, his steps slow and careful now that he was right where his enemy wanted him. That he had to exercise such caution in his own woods was infuriating—somehow these elves had managed to slip past the border undetected.

Still, the elves didn't know the land like Lucyan did. He'd been hunting in these woods with his brothers since they were old enough to hold a bow and arrow. He knew this place like the back of his hand—that knowledge, plus his superior senses, made it impossible for the elves to ambush him.

Lucyan approached the clearing with confidence, but that vanished when he caught the elves' scent. Dammit. They'd demanded to set the meeting at midnight, so by leaving two hours early, he had expected to arrive before his enemies so he could scout the area. But they were already here. He couldn't see them, or even hear them, but his nose never lied. He could feel their watchful presence in his bones.

He thought briefly of the cloak, but if the scent repelled *him*, donning it would be the equivalent of waving a red flag at the elves. So, he hid behind a tall bush and waited.

Eventually, the elves arrived in a small, triangular formation —just three of them. They had come unarmed, as promised—or at least it appeared so. Hands bound, blindfolded, Taldren walked among them, a rope around his neck; the elf leading their party used it to herd him, to Lucyan's outrage. He calmed himself with the knowledge that, at least to his eyes, Taldren was unharmed. But then again, that meant little—the elves could have tortured him, then healed him afterward.

The group stopped in the middle of the clearing, and the head elf looked straight toward Lucyan's hiding place. "Come forth, son of Dragonfell. We come in peace."

Well, then.

He stepped into the light.

"You're the one they call Lucyan," the elf said.

Lucyan only nodded, not trusting himself to speak. He'd been wrong. The elven king hadn't just sent some noble.

He'd sent his own son.

Prince Ryolas, commander of Elvenhame's armies, was the elf that stood before him, not some lackey. He hadn't even attempted to hide his identity—he wore no hood to hide his features, and his shining gold and green helm had the stag's antlers jutting from both sides: the commander's sigil. His matching armor was highly polished, but Lucyan could pick out the small dents with his keen eyes. This was a man of action, not one who hid behind his armies.

"So, you've come in your coward father's stead," Lucyan said. "Shall I send your head back to him as a present?"

Ryolas sighed. "You couldn't if you tried," he said. "But I have not come to fight, in any case. I have come to talk."

"There is nothing to talk about," Lucyan said between gritted teeth. "Your father killed my mother. He needs to pay for his crimes."

"This blind hatred of yours is exactly why I've called you here," Ryolas said. "Although I would have preferred all three of you to come and hear me out."

"Tough luck," Lucyan growled. Hot smoke puffed from his mouth with each word, clouding the air in front of him as if it were mist.

The elven prince raised an eyebrow at Lucyan's barely leashed temper. "From what I hear, while appealing to your compassion may be a waste of my valuable time, I may yet manage to make you see the truth with logic."

Lucyan waited. Logic, he'd said. So, he meant to manipulate him. He wouldn't be the first to try.

"First things first." The prince waved his hand, and Taldren's bindings slithered away. The dragon born seemed confused for a moment; he looked at the elven king, who nodded his consent.

What were they up to?

Taldren walked toward Lucyan, looking almost as suspicious as Lucyan felt.

"Tell me you have backup," he whispered.

Lucyan didn't bother replying, knowing just how acute elf hearing could be.

"He does, I'm sure. He won't need any," the prince assured them. "You believed we intended you harm. You believed this was a trap."

"It is. You just intend to fuck with my mind rather than my body. Smarter," Lucyan admitted.

Ryolas smiled. "Hardly. I have summoned you here, and given you your kin back in good faith, so that you may hear me when I tell you this: my family did not organize your mother's demise."

For a moment, Lucyan went entirely still, astonished. Then, he laughed out loud.

"Really? That's your play?"

It was so damn pathetic, he hadn't even thought the king would bother. His mother had been killed under dubious circumstances: stricken by some mysterious illness, though they couldn't figure out how, as dragons didn't suffer human ailments. Their father had done a thorough investigation, and all evidence had pointed to the elves.

"So, you've chosen to insult my intelligence," Lucyan finally said, his humor fading. "I recant my previous comment about your own."

"On the contrary," the prince said, unruffled, "I've chosen to count on your intelligence. I don't expect you to believe my words today, but eventually, you will. This conversation will stay in your mind until you reread the reports and see every little thing that doesn't add up. But first, you'll ask yourself why a race as wise as ours would risk everything to murder an irrelevant human who'd already served her only purpose."

"You know kings go mad without their mates!" Lucyan spat. "You wanted to destroy my father, his kingdom, and you've succeeded!"

Unable to bear it any longer, Lucyan finally opened his mouth, loosening his grip on the fire building inside him. It burst from his jaw in a torrent, scorching the air, screaming as it barreled straight toward his enemies. But the elven prince just waved his hand, and the fire disappeared, sucked into thin air.

"What the hell?" Lucyan yanked his sword from his sheath and charged. He didn't even blink when Alistair and Drystan burst from the trees behind him, weapons drawn. He'd known his brothers would figure out his plan eventually—the invisibility cloak was not to evade them completely, but to delay them so they wouldn't charge into an ambush. When he'd left the cloak on the ground, he'd also dropped a note.

Stay hidden until I call. You get to share the cloak. Don't let the wind catch its stench.

The clash of swords rang in the clearing as Alistair attacked one of the elves. Drystan crossed swords with the other, while Lucyan made for the elven prince. If they didn't want to tell him the truth, he'd *make* them.

"How predictable," the prince drawled, dodging Lucyan's first strike. He was fast, perhaps even faster than Lucyan, but it didn't matter. The elves had brought no weapons—they were done for. "Think on what I said, dragonling, and send word when you wish to speak to me again."

Lucyan snarled, swinging his sword down again, but it met air. The elven prince had vanished, and so had his entourage.

"What sorcery is this?" Drystan demanded, whirling about the clearing. Alistair sprinted for the trees, looking for the elves, but Lucyan didn't bother. They'd used some spell to disappear —he could smell the magic in the air.

"The more important question," Lucyan said through clenched teeth, "is what the hell did Prince Ryolas hope to accomplish?"

"He's obviously trying to plant lies in our head," Drystan said dismissively. He turned to Taldren. "Did they hurt you in any way?"

Taldren shook his head, his eyes narrowed. "They were remarkably civil. They could have tortured me, or thrown me into a dungeon, but they brought me here and gave me back. Why would they do that?"

"I don't know," Lucyan said, his voice hollow. None of this added up. If the elves were telling the truth, if they hadn't really killed their mother...

Lucyan shook his head firmly, dislodging the doubt. This was exactly what he'd thought. The elven prince was trying to fuck with his mind. And he damn well wasn't going to let him succeed.

FIVE

Come forth.

The words echoed in Dareena's head as she gaped at Tariana, who still smirked at her with that wicked gleam in her eye. Shock rooted her to the ground, rendering her paralyzed. Her mind froze, trying to process what had happened.

"Dareena," Tildy squeaked, nudging her in the ribs. "Get up there!"

The crowd broke out in whispers, all eyes turning her way.

"It's not possible."

"They chose her?"

"Surely this is a mistake."

"Why is she just standing there?"

That last one galvanized Dareena into action. She took a step forward, and as she did, she met Lyria's gaze. Her pale blue eyes blazed, her perfect teeth bared into a snarl, her face reddened with fury. She stepped toward Dareena, but her mother, standing behind her, snatched her back.

An unexpected smirk twitched at Dareena's lips, and she had to hold it back. Even the high and mighty Lyria Hallowdale could do nothing. The huntress had chosen *Dareena*, not her. The thought bolstered her, and she lifted her chin and strode to the podium to curtsy and take her place by the other girls.

As she lifted her head, she noticed for the first time that while Tariana looked pleased, the other soldiers' eyes were wide with shock. Was her name really on that list? They didn't look particularly happy to see her standing there.

Maybe this is a mistake.

"Congratulations," Tariana said to the three of them, banishing that idea from Dareena's head. For whatever reason, her name had been called, and as nobody was dragging her away, she was obviously here to stay. "The three of you are Chosen. We shall now feast and drink in your honor, for on the morrow, you will travel at first light to Dragon's Keep, where you shall participate in the Selection Ritual."

She smiled broadly, and the crowd, overcoming its shock, clapped and cheered. Before Dareena knew what was happening, the three girls were being carried off by the crowd, who were chanting their names. Dareena exchanged helpless grins with the other girls, and if they looked displeased by the fact that she'd been Chosen, they didn't show it.

The three women were carried to the feasting tent, where long tables had been set out with food. They were deposited at the head of the lord's table, and Dareena was inordinately pleased to see Lyria forced to sit near the foot of the table while she sat to the lord's left. Normally Lyria would have sat near her father, but since the huntress sat near the lord and his wife, there was no choice but to put her toward the end.

"I know you weren't expecting this," Mira said in a low voice. She was seated to Dareena's left. "But I'm glad they chose you instead of Lyria."

"Shhh," Cyra scolded from Dareena's other side. "She's only a few seats away from us."

"And so what if she is?" Mira tossed a skein of strawberry-blonde hair over her shoulder. "It's not like she can hear us over all this noise, and even if she could, there's nothing she can do. If she tries to interfere with us in any way, she'll be executed. The law is clear."

Dareena swallowed, glancing at Lyria out of the corner of her eye. She'd schooled her expression into cold indifference, ignoring everyone around her as she cut up her roast with a knife and fork. For a split second, Dareena felt pity for her. It had to be a shock, having the rug ripped out from beneath her, and the added humiliation of being forced to sit on the far end of the table...

Lyria lifted her chin and met Dareena's gaze with such blazing hatred that Dareena wanted to recoil. Her momentary pity vanished, and she gave Lyria a cool look before returning her attention to her companions.

"I'm sure she'll find a way to survive," Dareena said, reaching for her goblet of wine. "It isn't as if she'll have to go back to being paupers, like Mira and me. The real issue is what happens when we come back."

"She'll be waiting to exact vengeance on us," Mira said, sounding worried.

"I won't let that happen," Cyra said fiercely. "I heard all about that scene with the honeycomb vendor earlier today—Lyria got her comeuppance. She should have known better than to pull a stunt like that the day of the festival."

Dareena shrugged. "She thinks she's infallible," she said. "At least her mistake means I get to see the Dragon's Keep. I never would have had this opportunity otherwise."

Cyra's gaze softened. "I am truly happy for you," she said, patting Dareena's hand beneath the table.

The sincerity in her tone melted Dareena's reservations, and she finally relaxed.

"Whatever the reason," Cyra continued, "the gods chose to bless both of you today. It isn't every day that common folk get to visit the Dragon's Keep and dine with the royal family."

"Why *do* you think you were Chosen?" Mira asked Dareena, leaning in a bit closer. "Did you make friends with the huntress?"

"I think that lovely dress had something to do with it," Cyra said, running a finger down the seam in her sleeve. "You turned quite a few heads today."

"Lady Tariana did talk to me for a moment," Dareena admitted, eyeing the huntress. She sat a little farther up the table, embroiled in conversation with the lord, who didn't look very happy. Dareena had a feeling he would be having words with the general about her choice later on, once they were in private. "She seemed to want to know what I thought of Lyria. I don't think she likes her very much."

Cyra raised her perfect eyebrows. "I don't see how a huntress could possibly have a grudge against Lord Hallowdale's daughter," she said. "It isn't as if the king or his family visit Hallowdale, and I don't think Lyria's ever visited Dragon's Keep."

"Maybe Lyria did something to slight her yesterday," Mira suggested. "Dragons are known to have quick tempers—Lady Tariana could have decided Lyria wasn't worthy and chose Dareena to spite her."

Dareena bit her lip. "I'm not sure why, but it feels odd to think I'm simply a pawn in someone else's revenge."

Cyra laughed. "Dareena, we are *all* pawns in this grand game of chess. The sooner you realize that, the easier your life will become."

Dareena frowned. "And just what do you mean by that?"

"I mean," Cyra said, her normally gentle voice growing dark with warning, "that if you think any of us are going to enjoy any kind of autonomy when we arrive at Dragon's Keep, you are going to have a horrid time. Whichever of us gets chosen as the Dragon's Gift will merely become a vessel for the future dragon king to pour his seed in. The Dragon's Gift will have to let go of all she was—her friends, her family, her past, however colorful it might be. She lives to serve, nothing more."

Cold dread seeped into Dareena's limbs. "Gilma," she cried, straightening in her seat. "Who is going to take care of Gilma?"

"You mean the old woman who lives near the edge of town?" Mira asked incredulously. "That's the least of your worries right now."

"I can't abandon her," she snapped, bolting to her feet.

Dareena had promised to check on her at the end of the night. How could she do that if she was stuck here?

"Excuse me," she said, bowing hastily as shocked gazes turned her way. "There is an urgent matter I must see to."

She turned to go and slammed into a guard's broad chest. "You're not to leave the table," he said sternly, clamping his hand around her upper arm.

A gust of wind whipped past her, and the next thing she knew, Tariana stood next to her. "And *you* are not to lay a hand on any of the Chosen," she said in a soft but menacing voice.

"Lady Tariana." The guard instantly lifted his hands, palms up. "I meant no offense, but—"

"What do you think would happen," Tariana said lightly, brushing her fingers against Dareena's arm in the exact spot where the guard's hand had been, "if one of my brothers, or gods forbid, the king himself, found bruises on this lovely girl's arm? Do you think they would show lenience?"

"N-no," the guard stammered, his eyes widening as he backed away. He dropped to the ground, prostrating himself at her feet. "Please, my lady, forgive me."

"Much better," Tariana said. She turned to Dareena, and Dareena forced her mouth closed, which had been hanging open in shock. "Now, Miss Sellis, what is so important that you feel the need to abandon us in the middle of the feast?"

SIX

The next morning, the Chosen were bundled into a carriage, each clutching the small pack of belongings they were permitted. The huntress had informed them to only bring what they truly felt they could not live without—everything else would be provided for them once they arrived at the Dragon's Keep.

For Dareena, deciding what to take had been simple. She did not own much aside from the clothes on her back, her coin purse, meager as it was, and a silver ring with a white stone that had belonged to her mother. Her mother believed there was an elven ancestor somewhere in her family and that the stone, which had been passed down through the generations, held some sort of magic. Dareena had never seen any evidence to support that, but the stone brought her comfort regardless. She fingered it now as she watched Hallowdale disappear into the distance through the carriage window, wondering how long they would be gone.

It was a three-day journey to Dragon's Keep, and the huntress had not said how long they would stay, much to Mr. Harrin's chagrin. He had been very displeased to learn that Dareena had been Chosen, and he told her that since she hadn't obeyed his wishes when he'd asked her to stay, not to bother slinking back to him.

Now Dareena had *two* strikes against her—Lyria would seek revenge, and Mr. Harrin would never hire her again. At least her value on the marriage mart had gone up—all Chosen were considered blessed by the dragon god, and families considered any matches made with them to be good luck. But Dareena would have to find someplace else to live once she was sent away from Dragon's Keep. Even if she settled down with a nobleman in Hallowdale, Lyria would find a way to make her life miserable.

"Was your friend Gilma taken care of, then?" Cyra asked, interrupting Dareena's thoughts. She sat across from Dareena in the carriage, a solemn expression on her face. "I saw you go off with Lady Tariana yesterday, but I don't know what happened."

"Oh, yes," Dareena said with a smile. "Once I explained the situation, Tariana found someone to help." That someone had been Tildy, who had been more than happy to care for Gilma in Dareena's absence, especially when Tariana had pressed a shiny silver coin into her hand. Dareena had said goodbye to her that night, and it had been both tearful and joyous. She'd promised to bring Tildy something back from the capital once she'd returned.

Mira shook her head. "You are the luckiest person I have ever met," she said. "Everyone thought Lady Tariana was going to take your head off—instead, she helped you. She must really like you."

Dareena shrugged. "Maybe that dress I wore yesterday brings good luck." She'd packed it with the rest of her meager belongings for precisely that reason.

Cyra laughed. "You did look very good in it, but there's something about you, Dareena Sellis," she said, her eyes glittering. "Something that is potent enough to attract the attention of dragons."

Dareena swallowed hard at that, remembering that all too soon, she would stand before the dragon king and his sons. The thought of being scrutinized by the four most powerful men in the land, men capable of breathing fire and causing great destruction, was enough to make her skin grow clammy.

Despite her rash of good luck, Dareena held no illusions that she was to be the Dragon's Gift. She would get her moment to shine in the limelight, and she would have to be on her best behavior. The last thing she needed was to bring shame with her when she returned to Hallowdale. Lyria would be expecting exactly that sort of thing...and Dareena had no intention of giving her any ammunition.

"Oh," Mira sighed, pressing her nose against the carriage window. "Isn't it beautiful?"

Cyra and Dareena exchanged twin looks of amusement. It had been three days since they'd set out on this journey, and they'd finally arrived in Paxhall, Dragonfell's capital. As the carriage rolled over the bustling cobblestone streets, Dareena stared into the distance at Dragon's Keep, located at the center of the sprawling capital. It was majestic, constructed entirely of shimmering red stone and iron, with Dragonfell's banner flying from its turrets. She'd never seen such a grand building in all her life, and they were about to spend an entire week in it!

Soon enough, the cobblestones disappeared, leaving a smoothly paved road beneath the carriage wheels as they passed through the tall iron gates of the Keep. The carriage pulled into the courtyard in front, and a guard helped them to the ground. Looking around, Dareena hoped to see Tariana or the other Dragon Force soldiers, but they had already gone—presumably to stable their horses and enjoy a bath after the long journey. Dareena was a little disappointed they weren't here for their introduction to the Keep, but they likely didn't have time—she was sure they had to report to the king as soon as possible.

"Look," Cyra whispered, nudging Dareena's arm. "We're not the only ones to arrive just now."

Dareena looked where Cyra pointed. Two other carriages were coming up the road, each carrying their own trio of Chosen. There would be thirty women total, Dareena knew, from the other nine provinces of Dragonfell, and the thought made her nervous again. How many of them would be common folk like her and Mira? It was more likely that most were noble born like Cyra, and undoubtedly there would be a few Lyrias strutting about like they owned the place.

"What are we supposed to do?" Mira said underneath her breath, looking around. There were three guards standing by, but they didn't seem in any particular hurry to herd them anywhere. "Are we just going to stand out here all day?" She shielded her eyes from the sun, unusually warm and bright this morning, a sign that summer was fast approaching.

"I think they're waiting until the others arrive," Dareena said.

The two carriages finally made it across the drawbridge and up the hill to where Dareena and the others stood. Dareena studied the other girls as they descended the carriage, and her heart lifted a little—about half were noblewomen, with fine dresses and regal bearing, but the others were common folk like her.

"Has a commoner ever become a Dragon's Gift?" Dareena asked Cyra out of the corner of her mouth as the other Chosen approached.

"Once, I think," she answered, her gaze also trained on the competition. "But I don't remember who."

Once all of the Chosen were gathered together, the guards ushered them up the steps to the porch just in front of the Keep's enormous iron doors.

These were no ordinary castle doors, Dareena observed as she studied them. They were easily thirty feet tall each, with strange symbols etched along the edges. The handles on the doors were fifteen feet up and obviously ceremonial—they were much too large and heavy for any man to lift, even if he could reach them. There was probably some kind of lever or contraption on the inside that could open them if needed, but Dareena highly doubted they were used often. Smaller doors were set into the larger ones, and it was through these that people came and went.

As Dareena stared, one of the smaller doors opened, and a man in deep red robes strode out. He was tall, with a shiny bald head and a thick black beard, and while his face was stern, he did not seem unkind.

"Welcome, Chosen," he said to the women, spreading his arms wide. "I am Tarius Bellamin, steward of Dragon's Keep. I am here to go over the rules of your stay and see that you get settled."

The steward pulled a scroll out of his sleeve and reviewed a list of do's and don'ts. The Chosen were expected to be in the dining hall promptly at seven o'clock in the morning for breakfast and in their rooms by nine o'clock in the evening. After dinner, their time was their own, but in the mornings, the commoners amongst them were expected to take classes in decorum, and in the afternoons, they would all learn about the history of the dragons.

"While traveling about the Keep, you must be accompanied at all times," Tarius said. "You will each have a maid assigned to you, who is responsible for dressing and coiffing you each morning and will also serve as your escort to and from classes. There are certain areas of the Keep that are off-limits—your maids will ensure that you do not accidentally wander near them. Above all else, you are not to engage with the princes. They have been instructed not to go near your quarters or speak to you before the ceremony. Should you accidentally run across one of them, you must bow and smile politely, then move on."

"What if we should run into the dragon king?" one of the other girls asked. "What if he tries to speak to us?"

Tarius gave her a smile, and it was not a particularly

pleasant one. "King Dragomir may do as he likes," he said. "Should he request your presence for any reason, you must not refuse him."

Dareena exchanged uneasy glances with Cyra and Mira as a chill ran down her spine. What exactly did the steward mean by that? Why would the dragon king want to summon any of them? Would he single them out for inspection? Goosebumps rushed over her skin—from all accounts, King Dragomir was a fearsome dragon with little patience who, in recent years, had been known to eat vassals who had displeased him. The last thing she wanted was to end up beneath his fiery regard.

I guess I'll just have to follow the rules then, Dareena told herself as their group was finally herded inside. Not a particularly easy thing to do, as she had a naturally defiant spark. But she would have to curb that spark during her stay, because even though Tariana had taken a liking to her, and the steward did not seem like an evil man, she had a feeling that her life might depend upon it.

SEVEN

Alistair knew where his siblings stood; both believed the elven prince had lied through his teeth to confuse them when he'd said his family wasn't responsible for their mother's demise. His first instinct was to think the same, but he tossed and turned all night, sleeping badly. The next day, he woke up with a small yet insistent voice in his head whispering, *"What if?"*

It bothered him that he was falling for what Lucyan believed to be elvish manipulation, but each time he convinced himself to leave it alone, the voice returned.

What if he hadn't lied? What if the elves *were* innocent?

He ignored the question at first, but by dusk, he'd concluded that he owed it to the kingdom to at least investigate the issue. Because *if* the elves hadn't murdered his mother, then the war that had plagued his people for years was meaningless, and they ought to focus on finding the real culprit instead of wasting resources fighting the wrong enemy.

Normally, he would have gone to Lucyan about this—his brother excelled at applying the right amount of pressure on people to get answers—but he knew he couldn't. He recalled his generally collected brother's dark, dangerous look after the elf king had escaped them. Lucyan wouldn't be reasonable. He'd dismiss the possibility that the prince told the truth unless presented with hard evidence.

The official way was also out of the question: if he contacted the council, there was a strong possibility that their father would hear of it, which was *never* a good idea.

Alistair made his way from his chambers to the guards' quarters in the east wing of the Keep. There, joyous cries still resounded, so many hours after they'd brought Taldren back. The men had never expected to see their beloved captain again. Taldren had gone to war at the order of the king, but before becoming a soldier of the Dragon Force, he had been a member of the Keep's Guard.

Lucyan had talked Taldren into glossing over most of the story of his rescue. He was meant to have escaped on his own, because if Alistair, Lucyan, and Drystan were known to have been involved, their father would hear of it. And he would have known they'd kept their meeting with the elven prince secret. Heads had rolled for less around here, and Alistair had no intention of being a casualty of their father's madness.

Of course, their father wouldn't kill his heirs. Not when they were the only dragons left alive aside from him who could sire dragonlings. But the king knew many other ways to make them pay for what he saw as disloyalty. He could very well punish their friends, servants, and even some of their family to make them pay for it. Taldren had agreed that this white lie had been for the best.

"Where's Taldren?" he asked when he didn't find his cousin in his quarters. "I thought he was supposed to be on bed rest?"

The guard shrugged. "You know Taldren. Never one to be idle. He's donned his old uniform and taken up a post at the North Wall."

Burying a sigh, Alistair went to the North Wall to search for him. He couldn't blame Taldren for wanting to keep busy—Alistair himself often assisted the Guard, though officially he was a member of the Dragon Force. A trained officer and a medic, in fact. It chafed at him that his father wouldn't let him fight on the front lines—all he'd been allowed to participate in so far were some skirmishes with border bandits near Shadowhaven. But apparently his family jewels were too valuable to be risked at the business end of an elf's sword or arrow.

Alistair found Taldren standing at the eastern end of the North Wall, watching the forest with keen eyes. The same section of forest where he'd been turned over to them by Prince Ryolas.

"Alistair," Taldren said, blinking in surprise. "What are you doing up here?"

"I could ask the same of you," Alistair said, clapping his cousin on the shoulder. "You're looking remarkably well for someone who's been held prisoner in enemy territory for an entire week."

Taldren shrugged. "They kept me warm, gave me clean

water. The only torture I experienced was that salad rubbish they call food. I could definitely use a roast."

Alistair laughed. "I'll have one sent up for you."

"Much obliged." Taldren grinned, but the expression quickly faded. "I know why you've come, by the way. I just expected it to be Lucyan, not you."

Alistair sighed. In other circumstances, Lucyan would have been the one to question Taldren. But as brilliant as Lucyan was, he was blind when it came to their mother. Of the three of them, he'd taken her death the worst. Before her passing, he'd been a kinder man. Now, he saw plots and conspiracies everywhere, and he lived and breathed to come out on top of the game. That was what had led him to begin a career in espionage in the first place.

"What do you think?" Alistair asked Taldren. "Were the elves telling the truth?"

"They could have been," Taldren admitted. "The murder was never solved, however, and they have every reason to want you to believe they could be innocent. In two decades, you may transform into full-fledged dragons. The king may stay behind, but the two of you who aren't wearing the crown may be sent to war. And then, the elves have no hope of winning. Not against two flying fire-breathers with an impenetrable hide."

"So," Alistair said, "you think they lied."

"I think they would have good reason," Taldren corrected. "But it's still worth looking into. Do you want me to start an investigation on the sly?"

"Please. I'll also look into it, but I could use some help. This is hardly my area of expertise." There was a great chance this would lead nowhere, but at least Alistair could sleep easier knowing he'd tried.

"I'll get started. But I won't be able to prove much without demanding to see some documents or other evidence I won't have access to without authorization from the council."

Alistair shook his head. "No need to think so far ahead. We're not after all the answers yet. All we need is one little clue —just one—that could make us think the elves didn't do this."

"One clue won't hold much weight in the eyes of the king."

"My father isn't our concern," Alistair said, though he knew Taldren was right. "Find me something to go on, and we'll throw the bone at a rabid dog who never fails to dig up what he wants to know."

"Ah." Taldren nodded in understanding. "You just want enough to get Lucyan onboard. Good call."

Because if the elves *weren't* responsible, they would need to dive into a case that had been closed for years and pull a very, very small needle out of a haystack. And there was no way they could succeed without Lucyan's help.

Returning to his apartments after the exchange, Alistair called Ruver, his footman, and asked him to bring the news records from the months preceding his mother's death.

In truth, he didn't know very much about the details of his mother's death. Alistair and his brothers had been hunting in a remote region on the opposite end of Dragonfell. It had taken close to a week before they received word, and another for them to return. By the time they came back, the investigation had already been concluded, and they had been too steeped in grief and pain to question their father's findings.

But perhaps they should have. Perhaps this entire war was a lie, and the real enemy lay elsewhere. What if the killer was a member of their own kingdom? The idea of any of their own turning on the Dragon's Gift was unthinkable, but then again, there were rumors of a heathen cult cropping up around Dragonfell that disavowed the gods and the divinity of the dragon line. It was entirely possible one of them had done something.

The news was recorded in weekly gossip scrolls he rarely bothered with. Gathering them took a while, and reading them, longer yet. After a short and unrestful sleep that night, he was back to it the next day, yawning his way through tedious announcements. The warlocks of Shadowhaven had come to pay their respects as they did each year, and the elves had arrived the next day. His mother had apparently worn red to greet the warlocks and green to meet the elves.

Seriously? They wrote about her clothing rather than whatever political issues had been discussed? What a waste of perfectly good paper. The writer may as well have used it to wipe his ass.

Frustrated, Alistair nearly tore the scroll in two. Almost. But as his fingers hovered over a sketch of his mother, with her long hair braided and thrown over one shoulder, he thought better of it. Perhaps the newspaper had its use, after all.

"Your Highness?"

Alistair lifted his head, surprised to see it was almost sundown now. There was a cup of cold tea and an untouched plate of ham and bread next to him. Time had evaded him.

"You may want to look out the window," Ruver said.

Alistair rolled his eyes. The man always was so expressionless, it was hard to tell whether he'd see the city on fire or a parade of naked women running down the street.

But as it turned out, reality was closer to the second guess than the first. Alistair grinned as he looked out the window—from his position, he could clearly see the group of women standing on the steps of the Keep, being addressed by the steward. There were only nine of them, but with their colorful dresses and long red and flaxen hair, Alistair had no doubt as to who they were.

Three of his sisters had returned with their Chosen.

By the dragon, was it only a few days ago that he'd been fretting over the succession? After everything that had happened with Taldren and the elves, he'd all but forgotten about the Chosen.

But here they were. Looking fresh and lovely as roses, and eager to serve.

Ignoring Ruver's protest, Alistair climbed out the window and walked to the edge of the roof to get a better look at the girls. As expected, they were all attractive. More would be coming soon—there would be thirty in total, all living in the Keep walls for the next few days as they prepared for the feast and the Selection Ritual.

But one stood out amongst the group of red and gold. A raven-haired beauty with curves that went on for miles. At first, he'd thought she was a servant, as she wore a simple muslin dress, but that was impossible—Chosens didn't bring help to the Keep. No, she had to be one of them...and yet she looked nothing like the women she stood with. Nothing like his mother, or any of the other Dragon's Gifts ever painted or portrayed in the halls of the Keep.

As Alistair studied her, his loins stirred with lust. The woman might have been wearing a plain dress, but her posture was regal, and she was every bit as beautiful as the others. Her skin was like fresh peaches and cream, and Alistair imagined how it might look if he slowly peeled that dress off her, baring each and every delightful curve hidden beneath. She was a lush beauty, that much was certain, and his mouth watered at the very idea of taking her.

Absolutely nothing like the others, he thought as he eyed her. She wasn't a potential Dragon's Gift, that was for certain. But she would make someone a very fine wife. It was no secret that the king wanted his sons to start breeding with human women and have dragon born grandchildren soon. The very idea had seemed like a burden at the time, but Alistair smiled now. He knew that, of his brothers, he was the least likely to become king, but if he could have a woman like that to warm his bed for the rest of his days, he would die a happy man.

"Have you ever seen a Chosen like her, Ruver?" he asked the old man once he'd climbed back inside.

"Like who, Your Highness?"

He frowned at the servant, wondering if he was going blind. But then again, he hadn't been standing on the roof.

"The brunette. There was a brunette standing right outside the Keep. With a group of Chosen."

"Oh." Ruver paused, before repeating a meaningful, "*Oh.*"

"She doesn't fit the profile."

"Indeed. But from what I know of the laws, the Dragon's

Gift may be any human girl. Don't worry, Your Grace. Just because one Chosen was poorly picked doesn't mean there's no hope."

Poorly picked. Alistair snorted. Many words came to mind when he thought of how to describe that gorgeous woman, but *poorly* was certainly not one of them.

EIGHT

I t only took three days for Dareena to start breaking the rules.

The first day was a whirlwind of activity. Dareena was shown to her room and assigned a maid—a shy blonde with doe eyes named Rona—who immediately took her measurements for dresses, then drew her a bath. Soaking in that small silver tub while Rona lathered her hair had been the single most blissful experience of Dareena's life—while she'd had baths before, they'd been in small wooden tubs barely able to fit her body, and the bathwater had never been this fragrant or soothing.

Afterward, the maid dressed her in a day gown of sky blue, with matching slippers, then brushed and plaited her hair. Rona informed her that while her gown for the Selection Ritual had yet to be made, there were a number of dresses hanging in her closet that would fit reasonably well and would serve for her lessons with the tutors. She'd then been sent down to supper, which turned out to be an impromptu lesson on table manners and the proper use of cutlery.

"That, Sora, is a butter knife," Lady Maude, one of the noblewomen who'd been assigned to train the Chosen, said coldly as she stopped in front of one of the girls. "It is used to spread butter over your bread, not hack at your meat and spray juices all over your dress."

"Oh," Sora said, blinking in surprise. "No wonder it's not working. I thought it was just dull."

Some of the other girls snickered, but they were cut off when Mistress Maude's icy stare cut toward them. "Anyone who makes such unladylike noises again will be sent to bed without finishing supper," she said in a clipped voice. "You are here to learn how to behave like proper young ladies. I will not allow you to embarrass yourselves at the feast next week."

"Why do you think they're giving us all these lessons?" Dareena muttered to Cyra afterward as they headed back to their quarters. "It isn't as if most of us will be living here. By the end of the week, we'll be headed back home."

Cyra shrugged. "I think the king doesn't want to be bothered on the night of the ritual feast by any of us acting out or having bad manners," she said. "He expects us to act like proper ladies even though many of us come from common stock."

Dareena smiled, noting that she'd said "many of *us*," not "many of *you*." Cyra truly was the epitome of grace and kindness.

Over the next few days, Dareena watched as Cyra gently helped many of the other girls with their lessons, often reading history passages to the illiterate ones in a corner of the classroom. The ladies training the young women approved of her initiative, and Cyra was quickly assigned to give reading lessons to those who needed them. None of these girls would be literate by the time they left, but at the very least they might be able to read simple notes or directions, which was more than they would have gotten on their own. Dareena found herself hoping that Cyra was the Dragon's Gift; she certainly deserved the honor far more than anyone else, as far as Dareena was concerned.

For the most part, Dareena kept her head down and did what she was told. Since she was perfectly literate from her time as Mr. Harrin's assistant, she could read on her own, and picked up the etiquette lessons quickly enough. But soon she found herself bored, far ahead in her reading assignments than the others. With little to do on her own time but wander her wing of the Keep and chat with the other girls, she soon began to go stir-crazy.

"Please, Rona," she begged one evening as the maid brushed out her hair. "Just this once."

"Absolutely not," Rona said firmly. "If anyone caught you, I'd be punished!"

"Just for tonight." Dareena caught Rona's hand and gave the maid her best puppy-dog look. "I'm not going to get into any trouble, I promise. I just want to sit in the garden for a little while."

"Oh, all right," Rona relented. "But if you get caught, you'd better not tell them I helped you."

Rona left the room, then came back a little while later with a spare uniform. It was a bit tight in the chest and loose in the waist, but it covered all the important bits, and that was good enough for Dareena. She waited until after Lady Maude did her evening round to ensure all the girls were in bed, then quickly donned the maid's uniform and slipped into the hall.

Dareena's years of growing up on a farm, sneaking up on chickens and rabbits before they could run off, had taught her to be stealthy. She moved quietly in the shadowed halls, her sturdy maid's shoes barely making a sound. There was a guard stationed at the end of the wing the Chosen had been assigned, but with her hair bound up beneath her cap and the darkness to hide her features, she looked like every other maid, and was disregarded. Heart pounding, she hurried down the stairs, then down a corridor she was pretty certain led to the gardens.

After two wrong turns, she finally found the right door and slipped through with barely a squeak of the hinges. Stars twinkled brightly overhead, and she inhaled the rich fragrance of roses and white lilies wafting from the bushes. The antsy feeling that had been growing inside her the last few days dissipated completely, and she felt lighter than air.

For a few hours, at least, she was free.

Smiling, she followed one of the many garden paths, walking lightly even though a part of her longed to run and skip. The moon shone bright overhead, nearly full, illuminating beds of tulips and pansies and the flowering vines that climbed up the garden walls. Straight ahead was an arched arbor of red-twigged lime, and beyond it were rows of cherry blossom trees in full bloom.

"Oh," Dareena sighed in pleasure as she slowly walked beneath the trees. Fragrant blossoms lined the path, and she reached out to catch one as several fell into her hair. The moon turned it a silvery pink, and she pressed it against her cheek, savoring its softness.

"And just what are you doing out here at this time of night?"

Dareena whirled at the sound of the voice, deep and dark and smooth as sin. She nearly toppled over at the sight before her—a man with raven hair like her own, dressed in a formal suit. He was at least a head and a half taller than she, with straight, broad shoulders. The lines of his muscular body were evident even through his elegant evening wear. His face looked like it had been sculpted by the gods themselves, with angular cheekbones, a strong, straight nose, and a hard, square jaw covered with a neatly trimmed beard. His thick black brows were drawn into a frown, and his full lips, which looked all too kissable, were pressed together in displeasure.

But none of this shocked Dareena. No, it was his eyes, a brilliant shade of amber identical to Tariana's irises, that stopped her heart and turned her blood to ice.

Oh gods.

"I'm sorry to disturb you, my prince," Dareena said, dipping into a low curtsy and praying her knees would hold steady. It took everything she had to keep her voice steady, but she fell back on the speaking lessons from the noblewomen, who had taught them how to modulate their voices so that they would not offend the dragon king or his sons with speech that grated on the ear. "I just wanted to enjoy the garden."

"No one is allowed unchaperoned on the grounds, especially after dark," the prince said sternly. "Come, I'll take you back to your quarters."

"N-no," Dareena stammered, straightening hastily. As she did, her cap came off, and her long hair tumbled free from the loose knot she'd tied it in before stuffing it beneath the white muslin.

The prince froze, his nostrils flaring. Those amber eyes of his darkened, and Dareena's heart, already hammering in her chest, erupted into a frenzy as he stepped toward her.

"I don't recognize your scent," he murmured, slipping a hand beneath her chin. Terror froze Dareena's throat, and she could barely draw a breath. "I admit to not knowing all the maids by sight, but your scent is new...and the fragrance I smell on you is not the common soap that the servants use."

He leaned in and took a deep whiff, his nose brushing against the sensitive spot right beneath her ear. Dareena jerked —it was as if a bolt of lightning had hit her, searing her nerve endings and igniting a flame inside her. Goosebumps broke out over her skin, and it took everything in her not to spin on her heel and run away.

If Dareena had learned anything from living in the country-side, it was never to run from a predator. And dragons...well, they were the fiercest predator there was.

"No," the prince murmured, his warm breath ghosting across her flesh like an invisible caress. She sucked in a sharp breath and inhaled the prince's own scent—it was rich and masculine, and tingles raced across her skin. "You are not a maid at all." His big hands clamped around her shoulders. "What are you, then?" he growled. "Some elven spy? Speak, girl—I'll know if you're lying!"

"No!" Dareena gasped. "I...I'm one of the Chosen!"

The prince instantly recoiled. *"The Chosen?"* he echoed, his eyes wide. "But you..."

"I'm the wrong color, I know," she snapped. "I assure you, Lady Maude and the other noblewomen training us have not failed to remind me."

The prince stared at her for a long moment before he finally blew out a breath. "Fine. Let's get you back inside now, before anyone sees. The last thing you need is for the ladies to catch you out of bed, least of all with me."

Dareena wanted to object, but the tone in the prince's voice brooked no argument. Besides, he was right—Lady Maude would have a conniption if she knew that Dareena had encountered one of the princes before the ball. She allowed him to march her back to her room, and though his face was taut with anger, the grip on her hand was gentle enough. If she didn't look up at him, she could almost imagine that they were lovers, taking a stroll—albeit a brisk one—through the castle at night.

Finally, they arrived outside her room. He pushed the door open, then leaned inside, his nostrils flaring. "The room does smell like you," he said grudgingly. "You've told the truth, then."

Dareena bit back a sharp retort, not wanting to anger the prince further. But she struggled against him as he ushered her inside, not wanting this to be over just yet.

"Wait." She wedged herself in the doorjamb before he could close it completely. "At least tell me your name." How could she possibly end this encounter without knowing which prince she'd run into?

His eyes glimmered as he hesitated for a fraction of a second. "Drystan," he said. "Now go to bed."

He closed the door in her face, and Dareena flopped onto her bed, a grin quickly overtaking her face despite the fear still pounding in her veins. She'd had a run-in with one of the princes and had not made an utter fool of herself! And moreover, he was incredibly handsome. She wondered if his brothers were equally so—they had to be, since they were triplets, but she had been told they were not identical, so she had no idea what they would look like. Tariana and her sisters all shared the same amber eyes, and she imagined it was a dragon trait. But what else did the brothers share? If the other two were anything like Drystan, they would be imposing—Drystan had seemed to suck all the air out of the space when he'd approached Dareena. Every inch of that man oozed with power.

Sighing, she pulled off her clothes and slid beneath the sheets. But sleep was a long time coming—all she could see when she closed her eyes was Drystan's handsome face, and her heart pounded once more at the strange feelings he'd stirred in her when he'd leaned in to sniff her neck. Gods, that man was magnetic. And there were two more like him...

As Dareena slipped off to sleep, it dawned on her that she might not be content with sampling this small slice of royal life. Whichever of the Chosen turned out to be the Dragon's Gift would be one lucky woman, and for the first time, Dareena envied whoever that woman would be.

NINE

A listair was in a sour mood when he came to dinner.

It was customary for the royal family to dine together at least once per week. Oftentimes they were too busy to do so, especially during this time of war, but the king insisted on gathering his family around him periodically. Alistair liked to think it was about tradition—family dinners used to be cozy gatherings where everyone would trade stories about what they had been up to during the week, and they would all laugh and trade jokes. It was the one time the brothers really got to see their sisters, since most of the time their paths did not cross.

But this family dinner was full of tension. The only sound in the dining room was that of knives and forks scraping across plates and throats swallowing the food and drink piled before them. For once, all thirteen siblings were gathered around the table—these days, Tariana was the only one who usually made it back from the fighting, while the others continued to captain their squadrons. But their father had pulled them all back from the fighting for the Dragon's Hunt. It had always been tradition for the king's female offspring to lead the Hunt, and even the war hadn't convinced their father to break that tradition.

"So," the king said after he'd swallowed a mouthful of roast beef. All eyes turned to him. "I see that you have concluded a very successful Hunt, my daughters."

Alistair's sisters bowed their heads. "It was an honor to serve the kingdom, as always," Zaria, the third eldest, said. She was the biggest suck-up, always the quickest to jump to their father's tune, and she nursed a grudge against Tariana, who was their father's favorite. "The Lord of Rowanvale sends his regards, along with a gift that I had delivered to your office."

"Which I received," the king said with a pleased smile that made Zaria's chest puff with pride. But the levity from his expression faded away, and he swept his narrowed gaze over them. "I noticed that there is one amongst the Chosen who does not fit the preferred guidelines. A woman with coal-black hair. Who amongst you selected her?"

The room fell silent. "She was my choice," Tariana said, and all eyes fell on her.

"Your choice?" Their father scowled at her, and Alistair noticed Zaria's lips twitch as she tried to hide a smirk. No doubt she was pleased that, for once, their father looked on Tariana with disfavor. "I thought you had more sense than that, Tariana. Is this why we have not yet crushed those elven scum?" he demanded. "Because you are incompetent? Did I make a mistake in making you my general?"

"Of course not," Tariana said, unfazed by the outburst. Alistair admired the way she kept her composure—everyone else in the room had stiffened. "There is nothing written in any of our scrolls or texts that says the Dragon's Gift must have particular features. Even so, I did not initially intend to pick that girl. My intention was to choose Lord Hallowdale's daughter, Lyria. She fits the parameters exactly—perfect figure, beautiful face, long, flame-red hair."

"Then why is she not standing in my Keep right now?" the king sputtered.

"Because she is an impudent little bitch, and she would make a terrible consort for any of our brothers," Tariana retorted, her eyes flaring. "She struts about as if she owns the place and terrorizes her father's subjects. Dareena—the woman I chose—was the only one who stood up to her the entire time I followed her around. We cannot afford to bring women like that into the Keep. It would be an insult to the dragon god."

The king stared at her for a long moment. As the seconds ticked by, Alistair exchanged furtive glances with his brothers. They were all thinking the same thing—that their father was teetering on the verge, and was either about to punish Tariana or praise her.

Finally, the king threw back his head and laughed. "A perfect response as usual, daughter," he said approvingly. "You are quite right—the dragon king would never pick a harpy like that to bear my grandchildren. Clearly, Lord Hallowdale has not done a good job of raising his daughter. I imagine I will have words with him when he comes to court to complain that his offspring was not Chosen."

The siblings said nothing to this—everybody knew that Lord

Hallowdale would say nothing if he knew what was good for him. Nobody dared question the king anymore—even Tariana treaded with caution, pushing only where she felt she could get away with it, as she did in this case. The conversation moved on to talk of the war, and the sisters gave their reports. So far it was a stalemate, the Dragon Force winning as many battles as they were losing, but Tariana assured the king that the elves were beginning to tire and that Dragonfell had vastly superior resources.

"We will best them," she said with such confidence that Alistair nearly believed her. "It is only a matter of time until we win."

"Well, well," Lucyan said under his breath after dinner as they all filed out of the dining room and headed their separate ways. "I ought to thank our sister for making life around here interesting. I saw that girl the other day when she and the others arrived at the castle—she won't become the Dragon's Gift, of course, but she'll be a nice prize for whoever doesn't get picked, don't you think?" He clapped Alistair on the shoulder.

Alistair gritted his teeth, refusing to respond. The taunt was obvious—Lucyan didn't think that Alistair would be king. And perhaps he wouldn't. But he didn't need to speak about Dareena as if she were a consolation prize. Any man would be lucky to have a woman who looked like that, dragon or no.

"No response?" Lucyan asked as Alistair stalked ahead. "Where are you going?"

"To speak to our dear sister," Alistair said.

"About what?" Drystan asked.

Alistair ignored them both and hurried to catch up to Tariana, who was halfway up the hall. "We need to talk," he said, grabbing her arm.

Tariana's eyes narrowed as she turned to face him. "About what? If this is about refusing to post you on the front lines, I won't hear of it, Alistair. Father made it very clear—"

"It's not about the bloody front lines," Alistair growled. "It's about Prince Ryolas."

Tariana's gaze instantly shuttered. "Why would you want to ask me anything about the general?"

"Because," Alistair said as his brothers caught up, "I know the two of you used to be friends."

"Friends?" Lucyan echoed. He stared at their sister incredulously. "You're *friends* with the enemy?"

"Shut up!" Tariana hissed. She grabbed Alistair by the hand and yanked him into the nearest room, which turned out to be the linen storage area. Alistair wrinkled his nose at the strong scents of soap and starch, and Drystan actually sneezed. Tariana leveled scorching glares at each of them as she shut the door.

"Where the hell did you get the idea that I'm friends with Prince Ryolas?" she snapped at Alistair. "And why in Terragaard would you think it's a good idea to blab such a ridiculous idea out loud, where anyone could hear you?" she asked Lucyan. Her cheeks were bright pink, her entire body taut with barely leashed fury. A lesser man would have quailed beneath her anger, but not the brothers—Tariana might have been their older sister, but they were still the princes.

One of them would become her new king.

"I have to admit, I am curious as to what brought you to this line of questioning," Lucyan said to Alistair. "Does this have anything to do with the little visit the elvenspawn paid us?"

"I decided to do some digging, yes," Alistair said tightly. "After what he said to us about Mother, I had to be sure that there wasn't some truth to it."

"What?" Tariana's eyes widened. "You *spoke* to Ryolas? *When?*"

"Ryolas." Drystan's eyes narrowed. "You address him so familiarly. *Are* the two of you friends?"

"We used to be," Tariana said tersely. "The elven king and his family have been to court on more than one occasion, and as Ryolas and I were of a similar age, we ended up spending the most time together. But that was a long time ago, when we were children. I don't understand how you even know of it."

Alistair shrugged. "There are rumors that you and Ryolas were more than friends," he said. Indeed, he'd dug up that particularly juicy tidbit when surreptitiously questioning some of the older members at court. He and Taldren had decided to start by tracing back the political dealings between Elvenhame and Dragonfell before the war began, and lo and behold, he'd found this out. "You've danced with him on more than one occasion."

"As I have with other nobles, back when I was forced to attend such parties," Tariana shot back. "The one good thing about this war is that I don't have to deal with such nonsense anymore. Ryolas and I may have been friends once, but we are on opposite sides of this war now. He is my enemy. Now, what is this about you three visiting him? If anything, it sounds as if *you* are conspiring with the enemy."

"He kidnapped Taldren from the front lines, then infiltrated our borders and sent us a note demanding we meet with him to save our cousin's life," Lucyan said. "When we came to fetch him, your prince charming fed us a load of bullshit about Elvenhame not being responsible for our mother's death, and that we should look into it further." His eyes narrowed. "You've never been quite convinced that Father's findings were sound, have you? Is that because your lover has managed to pull the wool over your eyes, dear sister? Does his cock feel so good that you can forget how shriveled and wasted our mother's dead body was when we burned her on the pyre?"

Tariana moved so fast that Alistair barely registered it before Lucyan went flying across the room. He slammed into a shelf full of linens and was quickly buried in a heap of bedsheets as he fell to the ground. Drystan and Alistair stared at her in shock as she leveled a glare at Lucyan, her eyes blazing red as all dragons did before they were about to unleash fire.

"The three of you may be princes," she said in a deceptively quiet voice, smoke puffing from her mouth, "and one of you may very well become king. But I have bled and sacrificed more for this country than your ignorant, spoiled asses will *ever* know, and I will not allow you to impugn my honor or integrity. The next time one of you questions my loyalty to the king, I will send you to the infirmary in pieces for the healers to stitch back together."

"Well, that went well," Drystan muttered as Tariana stalked from the room. She slammed the door so hard, the walls actually shook. "I hope that was satisfying, Lucyan, because I doubt our sister will be speaking to us for the rest of the year at this rate."

"Good riddance," Lucyan grumbled as he got to his feet. "I could do with a bit less self-righteousness in my life."

Alistair shook his head, leaving his brothers behind as he returned to his rooms. Tariana was loyal to Dragonfell—there was no doubt in his mind about that. As a fellow soldier, he knew her better than his brothers, which was why it had shocked him when he'd learned of her connection to the elven prince. But it was more obvious to him than ever that their eldest sister was hiding something...and being loyal to Dragonfell was not necessarily the same as being loyal to the king.

TEN

"I don't think I'm ready for this," Mira murmured.

"Of course you are. You're going to do great in there." Dareena squeezed her hand, as much for Mira's comfort as her own, as the noblewomen ushered them toward the ballroom. From a bird's eye view, Dareena was certain they looked like a sparkling sea of silk and lace and tulle—all of the women were decked out in dazzling dresses worth a king's ransom, their hair styled to within an inch of their lives.

"That's easy for you to say," Mira groused. "You look breathtaking." She swept her gaze over Dareena, who wore a garnet dress with off-the-shoulder sleeves and a skirt with so much fabric it seemed to go on for miles. The bodice was embroidered with black roses, and matching obsidian stones winked at her ears. Her long black hair had been curled, and the curls gathered up at the nape of her neck and off to the side, leaving the column of her throat on full display. She'd barely recognized herself when Rona had finally turned her toward the mirror—in addition to the gorgeous clothes, her lips had been painted a matching red and her eyes dusted with shimmery powder and lined in kohl that made her green irises stand out even more than usual.

Amidst a sea of blonde and red and pastels, she was a jewel in a bed of flowers.

"Don't fret," Cyra said, taking Mira's other hand. She was dressed in deep green that offset her flaming curls to perfection. "You look beautiful, Mira. You're going to knock the princes' socks off in that dress."

Cyra skimmed a hand along the silken blue fabric of Mira's skirt, and Mira blushed. "I doubt they'll take a second glance at me," she said, her gray eyes sweeping through the other girls. "I'm just one of many."

"Then you'll just have to show them your stellar personality," Dareena declared.

"Hush," one of the noblewomen admonished them as they arrived. Light and music spilled through the open doors of the ballroom, and a crowd already milled about. Dareena's back went taut with nerves as she realized Drystan would be there. Her skin tingled, and she could feel his breath on her skin, hear his deep, seductive timber echoing in her ears.

Don't be silly, she told herself as the ladies ushered them in. *He won't even notice you in this crowd.*

The chatter of conversation dimmed as they entered, necks craning as everyone turned to get a good look at the Chosen. The place was filled to the brim with nobles, all dressed in their finery. Dareena hid her shock as she spotted Lord Hallowdale and his wife in the crowd. She'd been told that all the lords and ladies of Dragonfell had been invited, but it hadn't occurred to her that she might run into the Hallowdale family. Oh gods, was Lyria here?

"I don't see Lyria anywhere," Cyra murmured, echoing Dareena's thoughts perfectly.

"No doubt she couldn't stand to come." The smirk in Mira's voice was evident, even if her expression was as serene as a glass lake.

Dareena bit back a laugh at Cyra's admonishing frown, but the smile on her face quickly faded at the sight of the king. He sat on a throne on the far side of the ballroom, surrounded by a gaggle of nobles vying for attention. Even seated, he was clearly a big man, with powerful muscles beneath his finery, and cruelly handsome features. His amber eyes lazily assessed the Chosen as they filtered into the crowd, and though Dareena half expected him to call them forward, he did not.

"You may mingle for now," Lady Maude said in a low voice, "until the king calls for you. Conduct yourself in a proper manner at all times, and do not do *anything* to embarrass me."

Dareena nodded absently, barely listening—she'd finally spotted Drystan halfway across the room, looking just as devastatingly handsome in another suit. Two other men, equally good-looking, stood with him. *His brothers*, Dareena realized with a jolt of excitement. One was a redhead with wickedly handsome features, a bit leaner and taller than Drystan. The other was a blond with long hair and dreamy eyes, a bit shorter than his brothers and with a stocky build. The three of them had their heads bowed together, and they looked like they were arguing.

"Ooh," Mira whispered. "They're even more handsome than I'd imagined."

"They are," Cyra agreed wholeheartedly, her gaze bright. Dareena felt a surge of possessiveness, which made no sense whatsoever—she didn't know the brothers, and aside from Drystan, had never met them. "I fancy the black-haired one, I think. What about you, Mira?"

"The redhead," Mira said with a breathy sigh, a wistful look on her face. "Do you think he'll ask me to dance?"

"No," Cyra said, an amused look on her face. "I think he's about to ask someone else."

They all whipped their heads around at the same time, and Dareena's breath caught in her throat. The redhead had broken away from his brothers and was striding straight toward...toward...

"Good evening, my lady," he said in a deep, almost melodious voice, his amber eyes twinkling with mischief. He took Dareena's hand and bowed over it, brushing a kiss over her knuckles that sent a frisson of energy through her. "My name is Lucyan Dragonas. May I have this dance?"

ELEVEN

"Dance?" Dareena stared at him with wide, emerald eyes. "With me?"

Lucyan grinned. She was such a delightful little thing, that round, innocent gaze completely at odds with the lush, decadent figure showcased by the gorgeous garnet dress she wore. "Should I be asking someone else?" he purred, looking around the room. "I suppose there are others I could settle for—"

"'Settle' being the operative word," Dareena said, surprising him. She moved closer, her shocked expression quickly morphing into a confident smile. "You were right to snatch me up quickly, before someone else did."

Lucyan laughed, taking her into his arms and guiding her onto the dance floor. "You play the game well," he said as he led her into a simple but lively step. "I see why my sister took an interest in you."

"Oh?" Dareena's eyebrows rose. "I didn't realize you knew about that."

"Our father worked himself up in a tizzy when he found out," Lucyan said as he thought back to that dinner. A flash of unease went through him as he remembered the conversation they'd had with Tariana afterward, but he covered it up with a smile. "Thankfully, she is our father's favorite, so he overlooked it and allowed you to stay. Which I am quite grateful for, or I would never have had this opportunity to dance with you."

"As am I," Dareena said, inclining her head. Her green gaze swept around the room. "Your brothers don't seem too happy to see you dancing with me," she remarked.

This time Lucyan's grin was genuine. "They're just annoyed that I got to you first," he said, winking at Alistair, who had chosen to dance with a redhead in a pale blue gown. "While they were busy arguing amongst themselves about whether to ask you to dance, I decided to take action."

"Surely you jest," Dareena said. "There is no reason for the three of you to argue over me when there are so many other lovely young women to choose from."

"That may be so," Lucyan said, "but you are the only one in the room who truly stands out, and you are somewhat infamous because of the reason our sister chose you. It's only natural that we would fight over you, especially since this is our only chance to get to know you."

Dareena's bright eyes dulled at that. "I suppose you're right," she said. "I will be going home tomorrow, won't I?"

Lucyan winced inwardly. He could have kicked himself.

What was he thinking, saying such a thing like that on what had to be the most wonderful night of her life?

"I wouldn't be so sure," he said quickly. "You could be the Dragon's Gift, and even if you're not, you don't have to go back. Unless you have someone waiting for you?"

Dareena hesitated. "I do have a few friends back home," she said, "but my former employer wants nothing to do with me, and the lord's daughter has determined to make my life miserable since I was Chosen in her stead."

"Well, we can't have that," Lucyan said. "If going home is not an option for you, I am more than happy to help you relocate. There is no reason for you to suffer just because your life was uprooted due to a royal decree."

Dareena's mouth dropped open. "You would really do that for me?"

"Of course," he said, pulling her a little closer. Gods, those curves felt divine beneath his hands, and the way she smiled up at him—it was like someone had filled his veins with pure sunshine. "If I had my way," he growled, leaning in to take a deep whiff of her scent, "I would take you for my mate right now and plant many dragon-born babies in your belly. These child-bearing hips were clearly made for just that," he added, gently squeezing said hip as he spoke.

Dareena's cheeks flushed, and Lucyan's blood stirred as he scented her desire. Oh, how he wished he could whisk her out of the ballroom right now so he could lift up those skirts and see what lay beneath. Some women did not look as good with their clothes off—their carefully arranged outfits made their waists look smaller, their busts bigger—but Lucyan had no doubt that Dareena would look even better out of that dress.

"Alas," he continued, half-speaking to himself rather than her, "a prince is not free to choose whom he pledges himself to. We are bound to the king as much as anyone else—perhaps even more so. But just because my fate isn't your own does not mean I cannot help you with yours."

The dance came to an end, and Lucyan finally released her. "Good evening, my lady," he said, bowing over her hand once more. He brushed his lips across her soft skin, then quickly strode away, leaving her to stare after him. He didn't know what had gotten into him—Lucyan considered women playthings, and had never been bewitched by one. But this one was working quite a spell on him, making him want to take care of her when he'd never done so for a woman before. He'd best put some distance between them before he gave in to the temptation to take her back to his rooms and make her scream his name.

TWELVE

"I can't believe it," Cyra whispered as everyone sat for dinner. "You actually got to dance with one of the princes!"

"I can hardly believe it myself," Dareena murmured, still in shock. She was vaguely aware of the other girls whispering, many of them shooting dirty looks at her. But all she could think about was the way Lucyan's hands had felt on her, and the wicked twinkle in his eyes as he'd teased her. Gods, he was even more handsome up close, with that dark red hair and sinful mouth that had practically begged her to lean up and kiss him.

"What was he saying to you?" Mira asked as the food was served. "It looked like you two were having quite the conversation."

Dareena smirked. "He told me that if he had his way, he would take me for his mate and breed many dragon-born babies with me." A small shiver ran down her spine as she remembered how his hand had drifted to her hips. "Child-bearing," he'd called them. A blush heated her cheeks—she should have been insulted, she knew, that he was talking of her as though she were a broodmare instead of a person. But all she could think of was what it might be like to bed him. He exuded pure, carnal masculinity. The wicked curve of his mouth, the gleam in his amber eyes, and the way he touched her as if he was all too familiar with a woman's body told Dareena he would be an excellent lover. But more than that, he'd actually seemed to care about her. His offer to help her relocate after tonight had been unexpected, and quite touching. She wondered if the other brothers would have done the same had she told them about her situation.

"Dragon born?" Cyra frowned, glancing up at the high table where the royal family sat. Drystan and Tariana seemed to be in conversation with their father, and Dareena felt a hint of disappointment—she had hoped Tariana would come and speak to her, but she hadn't seen the huntress since arriving at the Keep. "Does that mean he isn't the heir?"

"Oooh," Mira said, practically licking her lips as she stared up at Lucyan. "Maybe that means I've got a chance at snagging him."

"Unlikely," Dareena said as another surge of possessiveness filled her. "He did ask to dance with me, not you."

"I was just joking," Mira said, sounding a little hurt. "There's no need to be catty."

Dareena flinched, feeling incredibly guilty. "I'm sorry," she said. "I don't know what's gotten into me." Really, what was her problem? This was the second time something like this had happened tonight. She had no more claim on the princes than any of the women here.

But then again, Lucyan *had* said he wanted to make babies with her...

He probably says that to every woman, Dareena scolded herself. *Don't allow yourself to get carried away by a pretty face.*

"It's a big night," Cyra said softly. "We're all under a bit of stress since most of us will be going home soon. Why don't we enjoy the food and drink while we still can?"

They all agreed to do just that, and spent the rest of the meal talking and laughing and comparing notes about the princes and all the experiences they'd had during their stay so far. Dareena was determined not to think about the ritual, which was coming all too soon—she knew she wasn't going to get picked, and as soon as the ritual was over, their time here at Dragon's Keep would come to an end. They would all pack up their belongings, and Dareena would have to figure out where she would go from here.

But alas, the meal could not go on forever, and soon enough, the king called for silence. "My lords and ladies," he boomed, his voice gravelly and full of leashed power. "It is time for the Selection Ritual, our holiest of events. Tonight, the Chosen will drink from the Cup of Dragons, and if the gods smile down upon us tonight, the Dragon's Gift will be revealed."

A reverent hush filled the room as the oracle, an old man in orange and white robes with silver hair and eerie blue eyes, emerged from the shadows flanked by Tariana and one of her sisters—Solara, she thought her name was. Dareena had noticed their disappearance from the high table at some point, and now she saw why. In his gnarled hands, the oracle held a giant golden goblet with dragons carved in relief along the sides. They approached slowly, the sisters humming a strange song that sent shivers racing across Dareena's skin. Their faces were solemn, their steps measured, and all eyes were on them as they approached Nalia, the gorgeous redhead who sat at the head of the table.

"Take this cup from us now, given freely in goodwill," the oracle intoned. "Drink from it, then pass it to your sister, to share in this holy wine."

Nalia gingerly took the heavy goblet, then brought it to her lips and took a small sip. The Chosen had been coached not to take too much—only a few drops needed to hit the tongue, and there needed to be enough for every girl. Everyone waited with bated breath to see if anything would happen, but when Nalia lowered the goblet, she was untouched by the golden glow that was said to illuminate all Dragon's Gifts who drank from the cup.

"Pass the cup on to the next woman, Chosen," the oracle said in a soft voice.

Nalia's knuckles whitened as they gripped the goblet a bit tighter, almost as if she thought if she held on a bit longer, the glow might finally appear. But after a second, she passed it on to the next person.

The minutes passed in excruciating slowness as each Chosen took a drink from the goblet, then handed it to the next. The girls did their best to hide their disappointment, but it was evident in the tightness around their mouths, and Dareena even glimpsed tears in a few of their eyes. Many of them were strung tight as a bow, including Cyra, who watched in avid anticipation as the goblet gradually came closer and closer.

Dareena, however, felt no such tension. She already knew she wasn't going to be Chosen and had made her peace with that. All she felt was a bit of sadness that this grand adventure was over so soon. She hoped that before she left, she would get to meet Alistair...it would be a shame to return home without having met all three brothers.

But then again, going home would also be a kind of relief. No longer would she have to watch what she said and whom she said it to, or suffer the constant presence of the noblewomen training them. Back in Hallowdale, she had spent most of her time working hard, but at least the few hours she did have could be spent as she liked, and she wasn't restricted from going wherever she pleased. Besides, now that she had been Chosen, her marriage prospects had increased drastically. Noblemen would eye her as a prize, since she was considered blessed by the dragons.

Even if her presence here had just been part of some silly game Tariana was playing.

"Dareena," Cyra hissed. "Take the goblet!"

Dareena jolted, and her cheeks flushed in embarrassment as Cyra held the goblet to her. She hadn't even been watching when her friend took her drink!

"Sorry," she muttered, carefully taking the goblet. The metal was warm to the touch and sent tingles through her arms. Was that normal?

It's just nerves, Dareena told herself as she brought the goblet to her lips. *Just take a drink and be done with it.*

Closing her eyes, Dareena let a small mouthful of the spiced wine flow over her tongue. As it did, a pleasant warmth spread through her limbs, slowly at first, and then faster as she instinctively drank more. She heard gasps from the crowd and hastily tore the cup away from her lips—she'd drunk far too much.

"I-I'm sorry," she stammered, then turned to hand the cup to Mira.

But Mira had her hands up, her eyes wide and her mouth gaping. "Dareena," she whispered. "Look at your hands."

Dareena looked, then nearly dropped the cup. Her hands glowed with a golden, ethereal light. No, not just her hands, she realized. That same light was pouring through the fabric of her dress, wrapping her entire body in incandescence.

"It is decided," the oracle said. Dareena looked up at him, and over his shoulder she caught the briefest flash of smug satisfaction in Tariana's amber eyes. "Dareena Sellis, the gods have blessed you. You are the Dragon's Gift."

THIRTEEN

D rystan stared at Dareena from across the room, struggling to keep his mouth from dropping open in shock. She looked just as stunned as he, and from the utter silence that had descended upon the room, it was obvious that everyone else felt the same.

As the silence stretched on, Dareena's cheeks pinkened with embarrassment. Her stunning eyes darted around, then spotted him. Drystan felt a wave of sympathy for her—he doubted she ever expected to be the subject of this much royal attention in her life, and now that she'd been chosen for the highest honor amongst their women, the place had fallen as silent as a graveyard.

Thankfully, the silence was broken by the king. He began a slow clap, his predatory gaze fixed on Dareena, and a moment later, the rest of the room broke into applause and cheers. Lucyan and Alistair raised their glasses to Dareena, and Drystan did the same, but his attention was still fixed on his father. He didn't like the way the king was looking at Dareena—as if she were a prize that *he* had won rather than a gift from the gods.

"Congratulations, my dear," he said grandly, rising from his seat. "Please, come forward."

Dareena slowly approached the high table, flanked by Tariana and Solara, their two oldest sisters. The oracle was right behind her, and while he'd looked stunned at first, his serene mask was back in place. Tariana's expression was blank, but Drystan thought he saw her eyes narrow slightly as the king took Dareena's slender hands in his own.

"The gods have blessed us with your beauty and grace," he declared. "Oracle, the necklace?"

"Right here, Sire." The oracle produced a velvet pouch from his belt. A lump formed in Drystan's throat when he pulled out a gold choker crafted into the shape of a dragon—the same choker his mother had worn.

"This necklace has been passed down over the centuries," the king said as he fastened the choker around Dareena's neck. It looked stunning around the smooth column of her throat, where the king's fingers lingered for a second too long for Drystan's comfort. "It was worn by Xandara, the first Dragon's Gift, and you will proudly wear it now."

"Thank you," Dareena said softly, her voice full of emotion. Her green eyes were bright as she bowed to the king. "I am honored to be joining your family, my king."

"And we are honored to have you," he said. There was a pause as his gaze swept the room, briefly lingering on his sons. "It is usually tradition to have your future mate dance with you on this night," he said to Dareena, though he was looking at Drystan. "But since we do not yet know which of my sons will have that honor, I will dance with you instead."

Drystan gritted his teeth as his father took Dareena onto the dance floor. The orchestra began a graceful, melodic tune, and the brothers watched mutely as their father swept the Dragon's Gift across the floor.

"I never thought I'd be jealous of watching my father dance with a woman," Lucyan said quietly halfway through the dance. "But I confess to a sudden urge to rip his throat out."

Drystan blinked, turning from the spectacle to look at his brothers. They appeared calm outwardly, but Drystan knew them better than anyone else, and he could see the signs of tension in their bodies.

"He is our father," Drystan said quietly, "and our king. To speak of him in that way is treason."

"We don't really mean that we would do such a thing," Alistair said just as quietly. "But do you see how close he holds her? It's as if he is deliberately trying to taunt us."

Drystan sucked in a breath. He'd thought he'd been the only one to notice, but if his brothers had picked up on it too, it was likely the whole room had. "He's probably just playing mind games with us," he said. "Winding us up for tomorrow's meeting."

Lucyan nodded. "I don't understand why he hasn't already made his decision on which of us will be his heir," he said. "He could have named one of us before the ritual and announced the decision tonight in front of everyone."

"Like Drystan said, Father is playing mind games with us,"

Alistair said grimly. "I just wish I knew the point of this particular one."

"Maybe he's just trying to make us more desperate," Drystan said. If that was the case, he'd certainly succeeded—Drystan's fingers itched to whisk Dareena away from his father and take her back to his chambers. He'd wanted to be named heir before—now he craved it, like an alcoholic craved wine, or a fat man chocolate cake. He needed Dareena in his bed. She was *his,* and no other man had the right to put his hands on her.

Not even their king.

The dance came to an end, and the king finally released Dareena. She came up to the high table to sit with the rest of them, a vaguely uncomfortable expression on her face. Drystan wondered if it was from dancing with his father or something else. He vowed to ask her about it when he had the opportunity to get her alone.

"Congratulations, my lady," Alistair said, somehow managing to grab her hand first. He pressed a kiss to her knuckles, his lips lingering on her skin long enough to make her blush. "That necklace looks stunning on you."

"Thank you," she said, her lush lips curving in a shy smile. "I honestly never expected to be Chosen."

"Well, I for one am very glad you were," Lucyan declared, kissing her hand next. "Of course, that now means my brothers and I will be fighting over you, but you are most definitely worth fighting for."

Dareena giggled at that, and Drystan shot his brother an annoyed look. "Fortunately, we won't be forced to battle to the death," he said, taking Dareena's hand next. "Our king will be deciding tomorrow which one of us you are to wed."

Dareena's smile faltered. "T-tomorrow? It is to be so soon, then?"

Drystan raised an eyebrow. "Would that be so bad?"

Dareena's cheeks flamed; she no doubt realized her mistake. "I didn't mean it like that, my prince," she said quickly. "This is just all so new to me—I really haven't had time to take it all in yet."

"Too right," Tariana said, appearing at Dareena's side. "Let's get you off to bed before these three ply you with too much wine. They are far too charming for their own good," she added with a smirk as she took Dareena's arm in hers.

"My dear sister, how is it that you manage to turn something that is normally a compliment into an insult?" Lucyan said with mock-hurt, pressing a hand to his heart. "We would never make the lady do anything she doesn't want to."

"And that is exactly what I am afraid of," Tariana said dryly, steering Dareena away. They watched as she guided Dareena through the throng and out the door, identical expressions of longing on their faces. None of them would be able to stop thinking about Dareena tonight, Drystan knew. Tomorrow morning's meeting could not come soon enough.

FOURTEEN

"Rise and shine, my lady!" Rona sang as she sailed into the room. "It's time for you to get ready for your audience with the king!"

Dareena groaned, burrowing deeper into the blankets. "I don't want an audience with the king," she muttered into her pillow. Her stomach was in knots just thinking about facing him again after last night. The way he'd danced with her, holding her a little too close for comfort...she kept trying to convince herself she imagined it, as he'd said nothing inappropriate. But she couldn't help thinking that he was *interested* in her.

"What?" Rona asked, sounding as if she thought Dareena had lost her mind.

"Nothing." Sighing, Dareena pushed the blankets back and struggled out of bed. She'd had two hours of sleep at most—after what had transpired last night, she'd been unable to do anything more than stare at the ceiling as she tried to come to terms with this new reality.

She was the Dragon's Gift. *Her.* Dareena Sellis, daughter of a simple farmer and lowborn serving girl, had been chosen by the gods to bear the dragon's sons.

The idea was so ludicrous that she burst out laughing.

"My lady, are you all right?" Rona asked, her eyes wide with concern. She took Dareena by her shoulders, which were shaking with mirth. "Do you need me to get you a tonic?"

"Please, don't call me 'my lady,'" Dareena said, waving off the woman's concerns. "I am anything but."

"You are the Dragon's Gift," Rona said in a tone that was part reverence, part admonishment. "I couldn't possibly call you anything else."

Dareena held in the protest that sprang to her lips—there was no use in arguing. "Let's get me dressed to see the king, then." She turned around so Rona could undo the laces on her nightgown. "We can't keep him waiting."

Either Rona completely missed the biting sarcasm in Dareena's voice or she chose not to hear it, because she simply hummed a cheery tune as she ran Dareena a hot bath, then dressed her in a gown of pale gold silk.

You've got to get ahold of yourself, Dareena said sternly to herself as Rona fussed with her hair. She had no illusions that Rona was loyal to her—the maid barely knew her. No doubt she would tell all the other servants about Dareena's ill-mannered tongue, and word would reach the princes, or worse, the king himself. She had to be more careful. No longer was she simply a serving wench—she was about to become a member of the royal family.

Even so, Dareena couldn't quite help the shiver of apprehension as she thought about meeting the king again. She remembered all too well how he had looked at her when they'd danced last night, his gaze cruel and calculating and a little too hungry for her liking.

"So, you are the woman my daughter brought back in her fit of petulance," he'd said, his hand curling a bit too tightly around her waist. "When I first saw you enter the Keep, I admit I was shocked. I had not expected Tariana to defy me so openly. But I suppose the joke is on her," he said with a smirk. "You are the Dragon's Gift, after all."

Dareena had ducked to hide the flash of ire in her eyes. But the king had gripped her chin hard and forced her to look at him. "Such beautiful eyes," he'd murmured, "full of green fire. You may not be what I expected, but you'll do nicely."

When the dance had ended, Dareena had been glad to be rid of him. After Tariana had dropped her off at her rooms, Dareena spent the rest of the evening with Cyra and Mira while the other girls avoided her—they felt as though they'd been cheated, and Dareena couldn't blame them. Even Cyra seemed a bit put out, though she'd offered her congratulations with a sunny smile. If Dareena had been in their shoes, she might have felt the same way.

"There you are," Rona said, stepping back. "All done."

Dareena looked at her reflection. The front half of her dark hair had been pulled back from her face and secured behind her head, leaving her face unframed while the dark waves cascaded down her shoulders and back. Rona had put a bit of rouge on her cheeks and a pale pink stain on her lips that made them look like freshly bloomed rosebuds, but other than that she had left her face untouched.

"You did a wonderful job," she said.

Rona beamed. "The princes will love you," she said. "Whichever one is chosen for you, I'm sure you will be very happy. They are all fine men."

Dareena's stomach filled with nerves as Rona escorted her to the audience chamber. *Gods, which one would the king give me to?* Drystan, with his brooding stare and stern countenance? Or Lucyan, who looked like he charmed the skirts off multiple women daily? And what of Alistair? She knew next to nothing about him, only that he was just as handsome as his brothers.

It only took a few minutes to get to the audience chamber in the south wing of the Keep. Two guards flanked the door, and they both bowed deeply, unsettling Dareena further. She steeled herself as one of them opened the door to show her in.

"My king," the guard announced. "The Dragon's Gift is here to see you."

Dareena's eyes widened as she stepped into the chamber. It was really a hall, she mused as she tried to take in all the splendor without openly gawking. She'd expected lots of red and orange, but the hall was turquoise, with a jade green carpet running the length of the gleaming tile floors. Golden arches lined the walls, interspersed with beautiful tapestries. Between the pillars, she could see the gallery, which was thankfully empty. She wasn't certain if she could bear an audience for this.

"Good morning," the king said, staring lazily at Dareena from the throne as she curtsied deeply. He sat in a gold throne raised up on a dais with the head of a dragon, its shining wings curved around as if to cup his broad shoulders. His sons stood to his left, below the dais, all watching her avidly, and his daughters stood on the opposite side. "Did you sleep well?"

"Very well, thank you," Dareena lied. She was relieved to see that standing amongst them was Tariana, who winked at her.

"Good. You may rise."

Dareena did so. She wondered if the king would force her to engage in conversation, but instead, he turned his glittering amber eyes toward his sons.

"I have brought you here today to tell you which one of you will be my successor," the king said to them, "but thus far, I have been unable to decide which of you ungrateful whelps deserves the title. None of you are fit to be king."

Dareena schooled her features to hide her surprise—she hadn't expected this. Drystan's jaw was clenched, and Lucyan look faintly annoyed. Alistair, however, was staring directly at her, an intent look on his face. Her heart fluttered as she met his amber eyes—he looked as if he were gazing into her very soul, trying to judge its merit. Quickly, she broke the gaze before she started to blush, and focused on a point just above his shoulder instead.

"Father," Drystan said carefully, "I think we all know that I am the better leader—"

"And *I* am the better strategist," Lucyan cut in, drawing a glare from Drystan.

"Schemer, you mean," Drystan fired back. "Our people are not merely chess pieces to be moved around on a board, Lucyan."

"Barely three seconds in, and the two of you are already squabbling like children," the king said, and the brothers immediately shut up. "What say you, Alistair? You have been remarkably quiet."

Alistair didn't even look at the king—he was still staring at Dareena. "I think," he said, his lips curving into a slow smile, "that we should let the lady choose."

Drystan and Lucyan both looked at him like he was insane, and Dareena barely kept her jaw from hitting the floor. "Let the Dragon's Gift decide?" Drystan said. "Have you lost your mind, brother? She knows nothing about any of this—how can we rely on her to decide which of us is best to rule?"

"A preposterous idea," the king scoffed. "Of the three of you, you have always been the most foolish, Alistair." He turned to Dareena, who was still struggling with her composure. "Which of my sons would you have for yourself, if I were to indulge this outlandish notion?"

Dareena swallowed hard. "My king," she said, glancing nervously at the brothers, "I would be honored to have any one of them." She didn't dare insult the princes by favoring one of them, in case the king chose a different one for her instead.

"Father," Lucyan said smoothly, stepping in. "I think it is a bit unfair to ask the Dragon's Gift to choose when she hardly knows us. Instead, I propose a contest."

"A contest?" The king's eyes gleamed with sudden interest.

"There is no contest," Drystan snapped. "I am the firstborn, and according to any law written back when there *was* more than one prince, clearly the rightful heir—"

"You are *clearly* talking too much," the king growled, his

amber eyes flashing red. The air heated several degrees, and everyone in the room froze beneath the king's ire. Dareena could barely breathe as she bowed her head—what would it be like if the king she stood before was in dragon form instead? Would she collapse beneath the weight of that wrathful gaze?

"Continue," the king said to Lucyan in a soft, menacing voice. "And be quick about it."

"I propose that you allow us three weeks to win the lady over," Lucyan said, sounding completely unperturbed by his father's mood swings. "All three of us have our different strengths and weaknesses, but what kind of kings would we be if we cannot woo a single female? Surely whichever dragon wins Dareena's heart is fit to rule the throne," he added, winking at Dareena.

Alistair snorted. "The only reason you are backing me up on this is because you think you'll win," he said.

"Of course I will," Lucyan said silkily, "but that isn't the point. The point is to let the lady decide which of us is the best dragon." He met Dareena's eyes. His gaze was like molten gold, and Dareena's mouth went dry as he gave her a smile that was pure sin. She remembered all too well what it had been like in his arms as he swept her across the dance floor...

"Very well," the king said, surprising everyone. "I shall grant you this silly little game of yours and allow the three of you to court the Dragon's Gift. Perhaps the competition will be good for the three of you—you all spend far too much time on your silly little pursuits. And who knows? Perhaps the Dragon's Gift will choose none of you, and I shall take her for myself."

"My king!" Dareena gasped, her mouth dropping open in

horror. She had been doing her best to keep her mouth shut, but this—*this*—

"My father has very poor taste in jokes," Tariana said coldly, striding forward. She took Dareena by the arm. "There is no need for the Dragon's Gift to stand here while the four of you eye her like a piece of meat. With your leave, Father, I will escort the Dragon's Gift back to her room."

Tariana turned on her heel, and Dareena clutched at her arm to keep from overbalancing. Relief swept through her as the huntress marched her out of the audience chamber, and if the servants and nobles in the hall glanced at them askance, Tariana pretended she didn't see them. They didn't speak until they were standing outside her room.

"Thank you," Dareena said fervently, placing a hand on the door.

Tariana said nothing, simply staring down at Dareena for a long moment. "You must be careful of my father," she finally said in a soft voice. "He is not as he should be."

"What does that mean?" Dareena asked, her stomach tightening with dread.

But Tariana only shook her head and pushed the door open. "Ring your bell if you need anything," she said as she ushered Dareena inside. "Do not roam around the Keep without an escort."

"Tariana," Dareena said, slapping her hand against the door-jamb before the huntress could close it. "Why is it that the king suffers your insolence? First, you brought me here, and then you marched me out of the audience chamber without his approval...I'm honestly surprised you're still standing."

A sadness entered Tariana's eyes, and she gave Dareena a bitter smile. "I think it's because of all my sisters, I resemble our mother the most."

And with that, she shut the door, leaving Dareena alone with her thoughts.

FIFTEEN

If he was entirely honest with himself, Lucyan had a hard time believing Drystan hadn't been selected to be the heir right from the start. For all his bravado, he'd believed their father would have picked The Dutiful One. Lucyan liked power, Alistair feared it—Drystan was the only one amongst them who saw it as nothing more than a responsibility, which made him the one most likely to be perfect in his position of power. And, more importantly for the king, at least, he would also be the easiest to manipulate.

But that didn't matter now. Their father had turned this into another one of his games, and Lucyan wouldn't go down without a fight. And the throne came attached to a gorgeous, curvy little thing called Dareena, a delightful bonus.

For the first time, there was a real competition between Lucyan and his brothers. They weren't to be vetted by wise councilmen or a mad king. Their fates rested with a young woman they simply had to seduce. Nothing aroused him as much as a fair fight.

Still, Lucyan didn't want to lose his brothers over the deal. How could he ensure that he would be able to fight for Dareena and become the rightful heir without alienating his brothers? Lucyan knew they needed to strike some kind of deal, an agreement between the three of them. Ground rules, perhaps.

With that in mind, Lucyan asked his brothers to meet him in his apartments after dinner.

While he waited for his brothers to arrive, he thought about the whole ordeal. He already had a plan in mind when they joined him. That was what he did: think and see workarounds, solutions to every possible issue standing in his way. Which was also why he'd make a fine king. Emotions could run high in dragons, and mistakes were so easily made.

The door opened, and his brothers walked in unannounced. "Well, you nailed it, brother," Alistair said to Drystan. "Father did end up surprising us."

"What else is new?" Drystan grumbled as he took a seat, making Lucyan laugh.

"Come on, now," Lucyan said. "Let us speak frankly here. You thought you were going to be picked, didn't you, Drystan?"

Drystan's shoulders dropped as he took a deep breath. "That's neither here nor there."

"Don't feel bad," Lucyan assured him. "I thought you were the clear choice, too."

"As did I," Alistair piped in, heading right to Lucyan's liquor cabinet.

"You've always been the perfect, disgustingly dutiful son.

Which of course should make you father's favorite," Lucyan said, needling Drystan a little. *Should* was the operative word. He didn't actually believe their father liked any of them all that much, at least not anymore. At some point during his descent into madness, he'd begun to see them as competition rather than family. He seemed fonder of Tariana than any of his other children, even though she was the only one who dared to openly defy him. Or perhaps it was because of that. Lucyan was certain that if a pair of balls dangled between her legs instead of lady bits, she would be next in line for the throne.

A silence stretched until Alistair finally broke it by setting a bottle of scotch on the table.

"Ah, I see you've found the good stuff," Drystan said as Alistair fetched the glasses. Their youngest brother wasn't a drinker, but after the day they'd had, they all needed it. He poured them all three fingers, which they downed before starting the real discussion.

"I assume we all want a chance to win over the beautiful Dareena and take over the reign?" Lucyan asked, looking at Alistair in particular. "No one wants out of the running now?"

His brothers' expressions were telling.

"Just clarifying." He wouldn't have put it past Alistair to nobly bow down and let the two of them fight it out, but his younger brother stood his ground. "Well, let's put all the cards on the table, then. I'm willing to do *anything* for this. Anything," he repeated, "except damage my relationship with either of you in the process."

Drystan's brow lifted a fraction, but Alistair smiled,

displaying no surprise. He always thought the best of people, and occasionally, he was right to do so.

"It's funny you mention that, because that's what I was planning to say," Drystan said. "We need to be able to stick together no matter the outcome. No matter which of us ends up on the throne, we will still need to consult one another."

"Agreed," Alistair said.

Lucyan wasn't sure about that. He wanted to remain close to his brothers, but if he became king, he didn't intend to consult either of them at every turn. He liked them too much, and the idea that his affections could cloud his judgment downright repulsed him. They'd need to take up a hobby and stay away from politics. Knitting, perhaps. Still, regardless of the reason, they agreed they shouldn't risk their relationship, and that was all he wanted for now.

"Very well, then. Here's what I propose. We all take turns courting the fair lady until she's chosen one of us. No stepping on one another's toes," he added when Drystan opened his mouth to speak. "We define a schedule and stick to our attributed dates."

Drystan and Alistair exchanged uneasy glances. Lucyan didn't really like the proposed arrangement, and it was obvious that his brothers were on the same page. Dragons were possessive and territorial by nature—butting heads against each other and fighting for her time was more appealing to them. But he'd said it, and meant it too: his relationship with his brothers was his priority. This plan might just save it.

None of them had been blessed when it came to family. They had sisters, but their inferior status at court had erected a wall between them. It wasn't that Tariana, or any of the others, disliked him, or were even jealous; they understood the reasons behind their importance. But still, they'd never formed a real, unbreakable bond. Their siblings were more like cousins—some of them, distant ones. As for the rest, their father was mad, and their mother was dead. When it came down to it, they only had each other, and what Lucyan had, he kept.

"All right," Drystan conceded.

"It does makes sense," Alistair agreed reluctantly.

They drank in silence for a little while longer, and after a beat, Drystan brought up the elephant in the room. "What about the... intimate part of the relationship?"

Lucyan winced, knowing exactly what needed to be agreed on here. Their choice was all of them keeping their hands to themselves, or all of them getting the honey pie.

"If we're to convince her she should pick one of us, I imagine we want to use all of our skills." Lucyan measured his words. "Besides, she may want to try on the trousers, so to speak. We must make a deal about how to handle that aspect of dating her. Either everyone is hands off or we *all* get to go as far as she'll let us."

He certainly knew what he'd prefer. Getting his hands on her lush curves had been on his mind since she'd swayed in his arms the previous day.

"I believe if she is interested, then anything goes," Alistair replied.

Drystan nodded in agreement. "I don't like it, but there's no other option."

"Then it appears it's all settled. We just need to inform the lady."

Lucyan smirked, remembering her shy, awkward glances. And now, she was supposed to be courted by three princes. A thrill went through Lucyan at the anticipation of everything to come, his hands on her smooth skin as she begged for more...

"No matter what the outcome," he said, "no matter what we do to win her over, and no matter who she picks, we stick together as brothers. No hard feelings, no fighting, no breaking apart our brotherhood."

Alistair raised his mug. "A toast, then. May the best man win, and we *shall* be happy for him. To brotherhood."

The brothers clinked their mugs together and drank deeply. The deal was done. When the next day began, they would be brothers vying for the attention and affection of their Dragon's Gift, the most important thing they'd ever fought over.

Lucyan sat back in his chair, trying to recall the last time he'd lost any game. He'd never lost to anyone when it came to wooing women, and he wasn't about to start now.

SIXTEEN

Dareena fully expected the brothers to come calling at lunch, but not one of them came to her door. She went the entire day without seeing any of them, taking her last meal with the other girls and saying her goodbyes to them, then spending the rest of the time in her room keeping company with a novel she'd filched from the library. Part of her wanted to go searching for the princes, but the other part of her wasn't sure she was ready to see them yet.

How in the world was she going to choose between them? Dragons were prideful and competitive, everybody knew that. If she picked one, the others would see it as a slight, and she did not want to get between the brothers. They were triplets, and though they'd bickered with one another in the audience chamber, she could tell they were quite close.

And none of that matters, a voice in her head said. *Because you are the Dragon's Gift. It is your duty to continue the dragon bloodline, and you can only do it with one of them.*

Yes. There was no getting around that. The brothers knew as well as she did that only one of them would have her. They had known this their entire life, had prepared for it, even if they were not agreed on which one of them should succeed. If this competition tore them asunder, that was not Dareena's fault. Their relationship was either strong enough to withstand this, or it wasn't.

Making sure the dragon line continued was paramount.

By the time morning came, Dareena had worked herself into a righteous fit. Did the princes really think they could make her a pawn in some game and then shove her off into a corner and forget about her? She hadn't seen them all day yesterday, and it was getting close to noon again.

"I'm not staying cooped up in this room another moment longer," Dareena declared as she toed on a pair of slippers. "Unless the princes have suddenly been called away to war, one of them should have come to see me. I'm going to seek them out, even if I have to go to their chambers."

"I wouldn't advise that," Rona said hastily, rising from the chair in which she'd been darning socks. "Especially when it comes to Prince Lucyan. He—" She cut herself off, her cheeks coloring.

"He what?"

"He...umm..." Rona pressed the tips of her forefingers together and looked away. "He likes the ladies," she finally said.

"Well that's not going to work in his favor at all," Dareena decided, turning away. She opened the door, then jumped to find Lucyan himself standing outside, holding a bouquet of red roses in his hand.

"My lady." He bowed with a flourish, extending the roses to her. "You look stunning this morning."

Dareena stared at him as she gently took the bouquet. The roses were fresh, she realized as she caught a whiff of their fragrance. Likely picked just that morning. "A lovely gift," she said, handing them off to Rona, who hovered behind her. "They might have been better received had you brought them sooner."

"My apologies, lady," Lucyan said, flashing a smile that didn't *look* particularly repentant. "My brothers and I were hashing out the terms of the competition, and we thought you might want to be alone for a bit after all the excitement anyway."

"The terms?" Dareena's eyebrows rose. "I thought the terms were already set yesterday."

"Yes, well." Lucyan scratched the back of his head, looking a little sheepish. "That was all very spur of the moment, and we realized that in order to keep things fair, we might want to set a few ground rules."

"And what are these ground rules?" Dareena asked, intrigued despite herself. How did the brothers manage to work this out in a way that they deemed to be "fair?"

Lucyan glanced around. "Might I come in?" he asked. "I don't quite feel that it's appropriate to have this conversation in the hall."

Dareena bit her lip. She wasn't certain it was a good idea to be alone in her bedroom with one of the princes, but then she glanced over her shoulder and remembered Rona. She had a chaperone—it would be all right.

"Very well." She stood back. "You may enter, but only for a moment."

Lucyan strolled right in as if he owned the place, taking the seat Rona had vacated. Dareena sat on the edge of her bed, not wanting to get closer—like Drystan, he seemed to suck up the space in the room, though not quite in the same manner. With Drystan, it was like he was instinctively dominating, but Lucyan...his presence seemed to curl around her, the way the scent of freshly baked pastries did as they wafted from the kitchen. Beckoning her to come closer and take a bite. Lucyan seemed to know it, too, from the way his eyes sparkled, and Dareena sat up a little straighter, refusing to let herself get distracted.

"So," she said, forcing her mind back on track. "What are these ground rules?"

"Well, the first thing we decided was that we will not all vie for your attention at the same time," Lucyan said. "We felt that was unfair to everyone, as you would not be able to properly get to know any of us if we were all talking to you at once or trying to ambush each other and spirit you away somewhere."

"Seems logical," Dareena said. "Is there to be some kind of schedule, then?"

"Precisely," Lucyan said. "We'll rotate between the three of us every day, so you'll never have to contend with more than one of us...unless you so choose," he added with a wink and a roguish grin that started up a bevy of butterflies in Dareena's stomach. Suddenly, she was far too aware of her position. It would take very little effort for Lucyan to press her back onto the bed and cover her with his big, hard body. Was Rona enough of a chaperone? Perhaps she should have an army of maids in here to protect her virtue.

"That's fine," Dareena said, brushing the feelings aside, "but I want a day off."

Lucyan blinked. "A day off?"

"Yes. Three days with each of you, then one day to myself," she insisted. "How am I supposed to choose if I don't have any time alone to think on it?"

"Very wise of you." Lucyan cocked his head. "Yes, we'll concede, though it will cut down on the time in which we have to woo you."

"All the more reason for the three of you to work harder to win my favor," Dareena said saucily.

Lucyan threw back his head and laughed. The light streaming in from the window to her left side illuminated his face, setting his red hair aflame and his white teeth gleaming. How in the world was it possible for a man to be so handsome?

"I knew I liked you." He stood and prowled toward her, her heart beating faster the closer he came. His amber eyes gleamed as they trailed down her body, then back up again to her mouth, and the next thing she knew, Lucyan had slid his fingers beneath her jaw. "Just think," he said, dipping his head. "The game hasn't truly begun yet, and I'll be the first to kiss you."

The smug hint in his voice penetrated the haze that had descended on Dareena, lighting a spark in her breast. "You think so?" she asked playfully. She pressed a gentle hand against his chest to keep him at bay. "Is it your day with me today?"

Lucyan sighed. "No," he said ruefully, letting his hand drop. "I'm afraid you're stuck with the boring brother first."

I⳿T TURNED out that the brothers had drawn straws, and Drystan would be the one to take her out today. The only reason that Lucyan had been the one to deliver the news to her was because he'd challenged Drystan to a game of roshambo and won. Drystan was waiting for her in the foyer, so impatiently, Lucyan claimed, that if Dareena didn't hurry down there he might well leave without her.

Dareena had quickly ushered him out, then had Rona help her change into a proper dress for an outing. This one was rose-colored, with a square neckline and bell sleeves. She was surprised she was so eager to see Drystan—she had not spoken to him since her brief exchange with him during the night of the ritual, and of the three brothers, he was the one who seemed the most mysterious. His stern countenance and brooding good looks seemed to beckon a woman, as if she might unravel his secrets if she could just get close enough...

"There you are," Rona said, stepping back—she'd braided Dareena's long hair into a side plait that hung down over her right shoulder, obscuring part of her collarbone. "Let's get going —you don't want to keep the prince waiting."

As promised, Drystan was waiting in the foyer for her. He looked tall and commanding, dressed in a dark blue and silver tunic that showcased his broad shoulders and back very nicely. He was studying one of the stained-glass windows, his arms clasped behind his back, but he turned slowly as she approached.

"You look beautiful," he said, surprising her with a smile. The curve of his lips softened the hard planes of his face, making him much less intimidating, though his presence still seemed to suck all the air in the space. Dareena immediately understood why Drystan thought he deserved to be king—of the three brothers, he seemed to carry the air of command almost effortlessly.

"Thank you, my prince," Dareena said as she curtsied.

"Call me Drystan," he insisted, offering an arm. "There's no need to be so formal. We are, after all, to be family. Although on what terms remains to be seen."

Dareena smiled. "Drystan," she said, taking his arm. It was so much bigger than hers, and yet it felt right, as if her hand, though tiny in comparison, belonged on his forearm. She hadn't expected to feel so at ease with him, not after that heart-pounding encounter in the garden, and yet as he escorted her out into the sunshine and down the steps to the waiting carriage, she felt none of the nerves she had expected.

"I hope my brother did not trouble you too much when he called on you this morning," Drystan said as the carriage set off. "He tends to run his mouth."

Dareena hid a smile at Drystan's annoyed tone. "He is a talker," she agreed, "but it will take more than clever words to ruffle my feathers."

Drystan glanced at her. "You are more than you seem," he said. "I apologize for the way I acted when we first met—I thought you were a spy at first, and then when you told me who you were, I was thinking only of your safety."

Dareena shook her head. "There is no need to apologize," she said. "I *was* trespassing in the garden."

"What *were* you doing out there?" Drystan asked curiously. "You had to know the rules."

"I did, and I truly meant to follow them," Dareena confessed. "But after three days of such a regimented schedule, being confined to such limited spaces...I needed to get out."

She expected Drystan to admonish her for her confession, but to her surprise, he nodded. "I too have moments where I crave freedom. I'm sure that might sound odd to you, since I am a prince, but my duties are just as binding as any woman's corset might be. My only saving grace is that I do not have to wear one of those heinous contraptions—I might be driven to murder otherwise."

That startled a laugh out of Dareena. "I think a corset would ruin your striking figure," she said. "You would look much better in armor."

Drystan grinned. "I do cut a fine figure in my armor, though the weight can be annoying. One of these days, I will be able to shift, and then the only armor I will need is my scales."

Dareena frowned. "You cannot shift?" she asked. She had thought all dragons could—the huntresses did, she knew. The Dragon Guard was formidable precisely because of their fleet of dragons.

Drystan shook his head. "Dragon males take longer to mature than females do," he said, reading her thoughts perfectly. "I will not shift until my fiftieth birthday or until I am mated. Whichever comes first."

"Ah." Dareena sat back a little. "Another incentive for you to win my hand?"

Drystan smiled. "You are incentive enough," he said, gently brushing his knuckles over the curve of Dareena's cheek. His skin was slightly rough, and his touch sent tingles through Dareena. "Any man in Dragonfell would be honored to have you as his bride."

Dareena glanced away, a blush tingling her cheeks. "But I cannot have any man in the Dragonfell," she said, staring out the window at the passing countryside. "I can only have one of you."

"And is that so bad?" Drystan asked, sounding a little offended. "We are not mere men, but dragons. There isn't a woman alive in the realm who wouldn't give her right arm to trade places with you."

"I do not mean to sound ungrateful," Dareena said with a wince, and truly, she didn't. What the hell had gotten into her? Just a few weeks ago, she had been seriously contemplating marrying a decrepit old innkeeper, and now she had three handsome, virile dragon males for marriage prospects. She should be jumping for joy.

"Then why do you sound like you would rather be somewhere else?" Drystan demanded.

"I don't," Dareena said, twisting around. She grabbed one of Drystan's hands. "It's just...what you said about feeling trapped by your duties." She looked into his amber eyes, unflinching. "There are few in the realm who do not feel that way, trapped in the cage that life has made for them, forced to walk the path that they have been set upon. I only wish...I only wish that some of us might have more autonomy. That we might walk to our destiny with open arms, rather than be forced toward it at sword point, or worse, race toward it in fear of what might happen should we choose to defy our masters."

The clouds on Drystan's face seemed to melt away, replaced by a wondering expression. "When I was told you were a mere commoner, I did not expect to bandy words with such a thoughtful mind. Are you a learned woman?"

Dareena shook her head. "No," she said ruefully. "I can read, but there is only one bookshop in Hallowdale, and those illuminated manuscripts are far too expensive for me to afford. The shop owner would not allow me to touch them. The only library in town belongs to the nobles, and commoners are not allowed access to it."

"We will change that right away," Drystan promised. "The Keep's library is at your disposal, and there is a very nice book-shop in town. We'll visit there, and you can pick out any book you like."

"Really?" Dareena's eyes lit up as a burst of excitement filled her. "You would do that for me?"

"You are my future bride," Drystan said, brushing a kiss across Dareena's knuckles. "For you, there is very little I would not do."

TRUE TO HIS WORD, Drystan took Dareena to the bookshop, which was even more delightful than she'd imagined. The place smelled like parchment and ink, and was filled with rows and rows of gleaming dark wood shelves packed with books. The shopkeeper was more than eager to help her, showing Dareena all the different sections, and by the time she left, she had purchased not one but three tomes.

"Thank you," she said fervently to Drystan as they left. "I can hardly wait until we return so I can read them."

Drystan laughed. The sound filled Dareena with warmth, the same way a good mug of ale might, and she found herself liking Drystan a little bit more. "If I'd known that books were the key to your heart," he said, his amber eyes sparkling, "I would have bought you the entire bookshop."

Dareena chuckled. "Let's go to the market," she said, taking his arm. "I promised my friend Tildy I would bring back something for her—I still intend to do that, even if I can't deliver it myself."

THEY SPENT the rest of the afternoon strolling around the town market, a large square filled with rows of booths. The clamor of merchants shouting as they advertised their wares mixed with the buzz of conversation. There were so many stalls, so many colorful fabrics and juicy roast meats and sparkling jewelry that Dareena was grateful Drystan was by her side. She could have easily gotten lost while wandering in the bustling crowd between the various vendors and probably not seen half as much as she had with him guiding her.

By the time they left the market, Dareena had collected a colorful shawl for Tildy, a woven blanket for Gilma, and a dagger for herself. The weapon had caught Dareena's eye because it was a work of art—the blade was finely honed, the jade handle fashioned to look as though it was covered in dragon scales. But it had been Drystan's idea to buy it for her, along with a thigh sheath—every woman should carry a weapon, he'd claimed, and the eating knife tucked in her pocket simply would not do.

"You didn't have to buy this for me," Dareena said shyly as they got back into the carriage. She pulled the dagger out of the small box the merchant had wrapped it in and ran her fingers lovingly across the carved jade handle. "The weapons merchant had much more practical options."

"Maybe," Drystan said, "but that was the one your heart was set on, and I saw no reason to settle for something less." Gently, he took the dagger from her hand. "Shall I help you put it on?"

Dareena swallowed, very much aware of how close they were—he'd leaned in, and his knees were brushing against hers now. "I..." She trailed off, glancing toward the sheath, which was still in the bag. The buckle was meant to be strapped around her thigh, and to do that...

"If you aren't comfortable," Drystan said quietly, "I won't push you. But I thought I might at least show you the first time, so that you can put it on yourself when you get dressed."

He pulled back, but Dareena gently grabbed his wrist,

careful of the knife. "I trust you," she said, even as her heart beat faster.

Drystan smiled. "I'll be careful," he said, setting the dagger aside on the seat. He picked up the dagger belt, then bent forward. Dareena bunched her skirt in her right hand and pulled it back so that Drystan could access her thigh. Her breath trembled as she bared her leg, and Drystan's eyes widened in surprise.

"No stockings?" he asked, lifting his head to meet her gaze.

Dareena shook her head. "Rona tried to make me wear them, but they chafe." She gave Drystan a sheepish smile. "I didn't think anyone would be poking up my skirts, or I'd have reconsidered."

Drystan chuckled. "Makes a man wonder if you decided to forgo underwear as well," he said, and his eyes darkened with lust. He placed a hand on Dareena's outer thigh, his fingers brushing against the edge of her bunched-up skirt, and for a moment, Dareena thought he might venture a little higher to test out his hypothesis. Sparks shot through her at the contact, and that curious warmth she'd felt before spread through her lower belly, along with an ache she'd never felt before. Suddenly, she *wanted* him to push her skirt higher, she *wanted* him to delve those fingers deeper, into places she'd never let a man touch her.

Was this supposed to happen so fast? Was she supposed to want to fall into bed with a man after spending a mere afternoon with him?

Drystan sucked in a harsh breath, and his fingers tightened

on her thigh in a way that made Dareena think their thoughts were aligned.

"Is something wrong?" she ventured when he did not move.

He lifted his gaze to her, and his amber eyes were glowing. "You are far too tempting," he said roughly, rising so that they were face to face. "If you were mine," he said, sliding his hand a little higher and making Dareena shiver, "I would be between your legs already, showing you pleasures that no other man could give you. You're already wet"—his fingers inched toward the center of her body, which pulsed with a need she'd never experienced before—"and aching. I could make that ache go away. I could make you soar higher and freer than any bird."

His lips were nearly touching hers, and she wet them nervously. "Then why don't you?" she asked breathlessly. His fingers were a mere millimeter away from her secret spot—all she had to do was open her legs...

"Because," Drystan growled, pulling his hand away. "Your thighs are clenched together so hard I don't think even dragon fire could force them apart. Your entire body is rigid with tension, and even through your lust, I can smell your fear."

Dareena drew upright, indignant. "I'm not afraid—"

"You are," Drystan said, gently now. "And you are right to be. I am no stable boy to roll in the hay with—I am a dragon, and you are not ready. I will take you the moment I have earned it, the moment that your body is ready to accept me, and not before. I want there to be absolutely no doubt in your mind that you want me, more than anything else in the world, by the time I slide my cock into your sweet pussy."

Dareena let out a shuddering breath at the image that

exploded in her mind of Drystan naked and between her legs, his muscled body glowing in the candlelight as he took her with all the ferocity and passion like only a dragon could. The next thing she knew, her lips were mashed against Drystan's, and the only thing in the world was him—his dark, masculine scent, the swell of his full lips against her own, the way his fingers dug into her thighs as he forced his tongue into her mouth. She moaned at the taste of him, and his answering groan reverberated through her, setting her aflame.

And yet...despite the ache between her legs, there was hesitation. She had not even gone out with the other brothers yet. Could she really allow Drystan to go this far on their first meeting? She had no doubt he would satisfy her, but would she be content, or would she feel regret for choosing him, never knowing...?

"As I said," Drystan panted, pulling back, "you're not ready yet."

Dareena bit her swollen lower lip. "You're right," she said breathlessly. "I'm not."

Drystan nodded tightly, then bent down again to continue what he'd started. Dareena held her breath as he looped the dagger belt around her thigh, but though his fingers lingered a bit longer than necessary as he tightened and adjusted the strap, he did not go further.

The dragon prince was a man of his word, it would seem.

"The blade goes in here," he said, sliding the dagger into its sheath. The cool jade handle slid across her skin, a startling contrast against Dareena's still-overheated flesh. "I admit this is not the best solution," he said, frowning a little. "I'll ask your maid to fashion a discreet opening in your skirts so that you can access the dagger without having to bunch them up."

"Thank you," Dareena said, surprised. The thought had occurred to her that it would be difficult to access the dagger, but she had been so grateful for it that she had not thought to bring it up to Drystan. "You seem very interested in making sure I am armed."

Drystan's handsome face tightened. "You may have traded your simple town for thick castle walls, but the world is a harsh place no matter where you stand in it. I would not have you unarmed should you find yourself in a perilous situation when I am not near."

The tone in his voice had Dareena frowning. "You sound as if you think that is likely," she said. "Is there something I should be aware of?"

Drystan shook his head. "There are no monsters prowling the Keep," he said, turning to stare out the window. "At least none other than the ones who reside here already. But even so, don't leave your room without that dagger. Not all is as it should be."

SEVENTEEN

Alistair prepared for his date, surprised by his eagerness. He hadn't believed himself to be a man of wild ambition like his brothers, but as it turned out, he was. This was a chance he'd never foreseen—a chance to win everything: the throne, the Dragon's Gift, his brothers' respect, and a chance to heal the kingdom, too. He knew Lucyan might not be mad, but his rule wouldn't be all too different from their father's, who was always scheming and looking over his shoulder, seeing enemies where there may be none. Drystan was a better option, but if Alistair became king? He'd see that no one died hungry on the street, and he wouldn't let politics get in the way of truth or justice.

They could say everything they wished about him being the lesser amongst his brothers; sometimes, it was a fair assessment. He wasn't as clever as one, as wise as the other. But in a fight, he could best either of them any day. He may not have officially met Dareena yet, but she was a young woman, and young women loved him as much as they loved Drystan or Lucyan.

He'd considered wearing something more formal for their first date, but he wasn't going to win this by playing the elegant card; Drystan was the one who excelled at that. No doubt his brother would greet her in an embroidered uniform. Instead, Alistair stuck to who he was. His soft, dark blue tunic fit him well, showing off the broad build women praised. He untied his hair, loose waves falling across his shoulders.

A stroll through the gallery, followed by a moonlit walk and a supper on the docks, he decided. It would be nothing like whatever his brothers would have chosen to do with her. And besides, that way, it would afford him the opportunity for her to get to know him, and vice versa.

He took comfort in the knowledge that being himself might work in his favor for once. Politicians might value the dutiful son, admire the cunning one, but the kind one was often vastly underestimated.

He was on his way down to the entry halls when a commotion caught his attention; the sounds were faint, but his acute hearing picked it up.

"What's going on?" he asked, stopping Tarius when they crossed paths. Whatever it was, the steward would know.

The man froze like a deer caught in the headlights—nothing he was supposed to talk about, then. Alistair sighed. It might have been nothing of importance, and in other circumstances, he might have ignored it. But the man's reaction suggested he ought to pay attention to whatever was happening.

Good thing he'd been early for his date.

Following the direction of the sound, he left the residential part of the palace, passing the guard post, the servants' quarters, and finally ending at what had been their stables just yesterday.

Alistair's eyes widened. He genuinely couldn't believe what he saw.

The horses had been taken elsewhere, and in their stead were a dozen makeshift bunks in each pen and a handful of visibly alarmed healers who were doing their best to be everywhere all at once.

"What's the meaning of this?" he snarled.

The healers seemed alarmed at first, and no wonder—in the rare occurrence when he did use that particular tone, he knew he sounded a little too much like his father. But they relaxed when they saw it was him.

"This," the oldest amongst the five professionals replied, "is the best I can do today, my prince."

"These men need to be taken to the infirmary wing at once."

"Four dozen men came back today, all wounded. There isn't any room to accommodate everyone, and those who were considered too far gone were to be left to die. Order of the king. I called everyone on leave today, and we're doing what we can."

Order of the king. In a perfect world, he could have been allowed to doubt that, to say that his father couldn't possibly have been that cruel toward his Dragon Force—many of whom were his flesh and blood. There may not be rooms in the infirmary, but they had dozens of empty guest apartments at any given time—converting one would have been an easy feat.

But Alistair didn't doubt it. Such was the will of their king and father.

The war had taken the lives of hundreds, if not thousands, of their soldiers, and it showed no sign of ending anytime soon. And all for what? A little while ago, the answer would have been obvious, but now...

Were the elves truly responsible for killing their mother? He and Taldren had found nothing to convince him otherwise, but even if she *had* died by the hand of an elf, had he been sent by their king? If it had simply been the work of a rogue, surely there was a way to negotiate an end to this madness. *Their* king seemed willing to come to an agreement.

"What do you need?" Alistair managed, sick with rage. They seemed to be working with nothing more than cloth as makeshift bandages.

The healer wiped a cloth across her sweaty brow. "Healing salves, alcohol, more bandages, water, a dozen pairs of hands..." She shook her head, exhausted. "We are stretched to our limit."

Alistair turned, already on his way. He strode to the infirmary, took what he could carry, and ordered servants to help with the rest. Going against his father wasn't wise, so he knew better than to reassign the medical personnel, but servants were another matter.

It wasn't until the clock tower struck another hour that he recalled he had somewhere else to be.

Alistair cursed under his breath, imagining wide, disappointed green eyes. But at the same time, he was grateful for the time he spent staunching the bleeding, cauterizing the wounds, and doing his very best to stop his people from dying on his watch. If not for that timely interruption, he might have lost sight of what this was really about. Not besting his brothers, not winning the favor of a pretty thing he'd never so much as spoken to directly. Who knew, anyway? There was a chance he wouldn't be able to stand her. Beauty was hardly an inclusive recommendation.

No, this battle for succession was about determining who'd run their kingdom and ensuring that the next king wouldn't be the kind of man who could order horrors like these.

"Let me see that wound," Alistair said softly, talking to a man who wasn't much more than a boy. While Alistair was no help with serious wounds, he could disinfect and dress the smaller ones the healers didn't have the luxury to attend to yet. And he could use his dragon fire to cauterize as needed.

"I see it's true what they say about Prince Alistair," the man said.

"What do they say?" he asked, to distract him as he cleaned the wounds rather than out of curiosity. He had a feeling he already knew the answer.

"That you're peculiar for a royal."

That was one way of putting it.

"Some say the country would be better in your hands," the man continued, dropping his voice. "That you might be able to stop the war."

He frowned, not sure how to respond to that. Could he? He would certainly try if he was in that position, but for a man he'd never met to have such faith in him...

He had started walking to the next injured soldier when a sweet voice pulled him out of his focus—a voice that reminded him that he was supposed to be elsewhere.

"Alistair?" Dareena asked shyly.

He turned to a vision in green; she stood there in a verdant dress that matched those gorgeous eyes, watching him.

"Dareena." Alistair inclined his head as shame filled him. "I apologize, the time has escaped me." He cursed silently—this was not the impression he wanted to make. There was blood all over his hands and his shirt—he was certain he looked like a vagrant right now.

"I waited for you a few minutes," she admitted, "but a servant told me I could find you here. She looked between Alistair and the rest of the stable, those keen eyes taking in everything. "You're a healer?"

"No, just another pair of hands. The infirmary is overrun, so I just...never mind. I'll go and get changed."

But Dareena waved him away. "Don't be silly. You must think very little of me if you think I would take you away from saving lives just so we can go have a bit of fun." Alistair stared, speechless, as she headed toward a basin to wash her hands. "Now, come and tell me what I can do to help."

Several hours later, Alistair and Dareena finally left the stable, exhausted. Dareena had worked tirelessly beside him as they'd helped the healers, dressing wounds, fetching supplies, and mixing up poultices. Only one of the soldiers died, and Dareena surprised Alistair by keeping it together through the ordeal. Many women would have been traumatized.

"I don't quite feel up to a day of leisure after all this," she admitted as they walked back into the Keep. He couldn't blame her, and he wondered if it was his cue to leave her to her thoughts.

But he found himself quite reluctant to let go.

"We could send for some music and talk in my quarters, if you so wished?" he asked.

Her emerald eyes almost popped out of her pretty head as she blushed adorably. "You mean, alone?"

He smiled kindly. "Not quite. There will be musicians, and my footman, Ruver, shouldn't be far."

She nodded. "All right. Music sounds lovely, actually."

He took her arm, which felt so small compared to his, and led her back inside the Keep. Catching the first servant he came across, he gave his order, sending for some food from the kitchens.

"How's your stay at the Keep so far?" he asked her. "That is, when one of your suitors isn't making you nurse soldiers back to health."

Dareena smiled at his joke. "Strange, for the most part. I'm used to being kept busy, so not really having any duties, having a maid of my own...well, it's definitely new."

He remembered the simple dress she'd worn that very first day, when he'd seen her upon her arrival.

"You're a commoner, right? I don't pay as much mind as I should to the talk around the Keep, but I believe my sister picked you?"

Dareena grinned. "That she did. Shocked me along with everyone else. But not quite as much as actually turning out to be the Dragon's Gift did."

He could imagine. "And how do you feel about it?"

She bit her lip, glancing toward him. "Honestly? A little trapped. Which is ridiculous, I know. Who wouldn't want to parade in finery all day and be waited on hand and foot?"

"A smart woman who values her freedom may have her doubts," he said, understanding her perfectly. She gave him a grateful smile, and he opened the door leading to his quarters, letting her go in first. His entry hall would suit their purpose nicely. He used it as a drawing room; there was a green and gold long chair where he did most of his reading and a few armchairs his brothers used when they visited him. Other than that, and a plush rug on the floor, the room was sparse and simple—he loved the open space.

Dareena made her way to his furniture. She looked like she belonged there, her dress the exact color of his chairs.

"Sir," Ruver greeted him, remaining perfectly expressionless when he saw Dareena. "My lady."

He turned back to him, enquiring, "Does Your Highness require me to return to the office?"

In other words, did he wish for some privacy?

He really, really did, but he shook his head.

"Not tonight, Ruver. The lady and I are to listen to some music—I know you're quite partial to violin. Please stay."

Grapes and cakes arrived, and shortly after, seven elegant musicians carrying their instruments. They played so beautifully his plan was altogether thwarted; he could hardly talk over the music. Dareena listened, mouth open, her hand over her heart, as if she listened with every part of her, leaning forward as though she could physically get closer to the heavenly sounds.

It was dark when they stopped.

"That was absolutely lovely," Dareena gushed, getting to her feet. "You are all terrific," she told the musicians.

"Thank you," the head violinist said. They all bowed as one. "We are pleased to hear it."

Alistair tipped them all handsomely, then sent them off for the night. Ruver also made himself scarce, surreptitiously slipping out the door behind them. He always could read Alistair's mood, and even though the prince hadn't said anything, he did want some alone time with Dareena.

"I've never heard anything like that before I came here," Dareena said. "I've heard music, of course, but at parties it's all about a fast rhythm to dance to. They were the same musicians playing at the feast, right? When I...when I danced with your father."

"Yes," Alistair said, instantly noting the way Dareena shrank inward, as if physically uncomfortable. "The same."

A moment of awkward silence passed before Dareena asked, "Do you three get along with your father?"

"Why do you ask?"

Dareena hesitated. "He seemed...confrontational when we all met last time," she said. "Almost as if he is jealously guarding his throne from you."

Alistair sighed. "Dragons are territorial by nature. It will be hard for my father to give up the throne, but give it up he must. He cannot rule forever, and now that you are here, he will one day have to step aside and let one of us take over." He took Dareena's hands in his own. "I realize you may have misgivings about us," he said quietly. "But you cannot speak such thoughts aloud where servants or nobles might overhear. The king does not tolerate those who speak out against him."

Dareena swallowed hard. "I have no intention of causing trouble."

"Good." Alistair smiled, then pulled Dareena to her feet. "Enough about my father, though. Let's replace that dance you had with something better."

"Oh?" Dareena giggled as Alistair swept her into his arms. "There's no music anymore, though."

"We don't need music," he murmured, pulling her against him. They swayed together to a hidden rhythm, their bodies moving in perfect time as they looked deep into each other's eyes, and for a moment, Alistair felt as if the stars were aligning. Without breaking her gaze, he guided her into the dance, and everything else but the two of them fell away.

EIGHTEEN

Late the next morning, Lucyan showed up outside Dareena's door with a picnic basket and what Dareena was beginning to think of as his signature roguish smile. He spirited her off to the rolling fields full of heather beyond the Keep, and they sat atop a grassy knoll on a checkered blanket to eat the lunch Lucyan had packed.

"Mmm," Dareena said around a mouthful of meat pie. "This is really good."

Lucyan beamed. "Cook makes the best meat pies around," he declared. "You won't find a better cook in all of Dragonfell."

"Oh, I agree that these meat pies are top-notch," Dareena said with a smirk as she dabbed her lips with a napkin. She was tempted to suck the grease off her fingers, but she knew Lady Maude would have had a fit if she'd seen such behavior, so she refrained. "But these strawberry tarts..." She lifted one of the sugar-dusted pastries to her mouth and took a bite. "They're delicious, but my friend Tildy's aunt makes pastry dough so fine it practically melts in your mouth."

"Well it's a good thing I don't live there, then," Lucyan said wryly. "I've a bit of a sweet tooth, and if I had access to pastries that good, you would be rolling me down the hill."

Dareena laughed. "Somehow I think you would keep your physique," she said, her gaze roving over Lucyan's body. He wore a dark green tunic and leggings, and the outfit was much more fitted than Drystan's, showing off his powerful limbs. There was no padding beneath that hose, she thought as she traced the outline of his calves with her eyes.

Lucyan grinned, seeming to notice her regard. "More than likely," he admitted. "I've never heard of a fat dragon."

They talked for a while about their lives—Dareena telling Lucyan about her life in Hallowdale, while Lucyan in turn told her about life as one of the king's sons. It turned out he had a knack for politics and intrigue—he was building a network of spies across not only Dragonfell, but elsewhere in Terragaard as well. He enjoyed the game of trying to figure out what people wanted and helping them to get it in exchange for furthering his own ends.

"Unfortunately, building a spy network is slow-going when one does not have access to the royal spy budget," Lucyan said. "I have had to make do by leveraging my position as prince and exchanging bribes and favors as I am able. But I do have a handful of informants now, and that network is only going to grow as time goes by."

"Why don't you have access to the budget?" Dareena asked.

"I would think the king would want to ensure you are amply funded."

Lucyan smiled. "He would...if I was working for him."

"You mean you're not?"

"Not yet," he said. "The intelligence is for my own use, not his, which is why I am using my own resources to gather it. I have found nothing I feel the need to share with my father, and I do hope you won't tell him about this. It's a hobby, you see, not an official career."

Dareena frowned. "But I thought he knew about this? You did mention being the better strategist when you were arguing with Drystan and Alistair about which one of you should be king."

Lucyan waved a hand. "I sit in on the council meetings often, just like my brothers, and Father often asks our opinion on how to deal with certain matters. Lately, though, the only opinion he seems to desire is his own," he added darkly.

"Your brothers have said similar things," Dareena commented, a seed of worry planting itself in her gut. Could it be that the king was not of sound mind and body? She'd heard whispers of discontent amongst her fellow townsfolk in the past, but she hadn't listened to them much, having little care in politics at the time.

Lucyan shrugged. "Fathers and sons always have their spats," he said. "But let's not talk of such things on such a beautiful day. What is it that *you* want to do? I've got you to myself for the rest of the afternoon—how would you like to make use of me?"

Dareena bit back a laugh as he waggled his eyebrows—she had no doubt in her mind as to what *he* thought was the best use of himself. "Since you seem to be so knowledgeable about the world," she said, trailing her fingers up his arm in a teasing manner, "I wouldn't mind learning about the War of the Three Kingdoms."

Lucyan blinked. "That isn't exactly what I had in mind," he said, sitting up a little straighter. "But you've certainly come to the right person. Why the interest, if I may ask?"

Dareena hesitated. She didn't want Lucyan to think she was worried, but after Drystan had been so insistent about protecting herself that day in the carriage, and with what the brothers were saying about their father, she couldn't help but wonder about the real motivations for the current war. She didn't know much about the histories between the three kingdoms, so it seemed like the best place to start was with the war that had driven a rift between them in the first place.

"It just seems that if I'm going to become a part of the royal family, it's something I should know," Dareena said with a smile. "I didn't have access to many history books, so I don't know very much about it."

"Well, we can't have that," Lucyan said. "Why don't we pay a visit to the library? It's always best to get history straight from the source. In the meantime, I can give you an overview."

They packed up the basket, then mounted the horse Lucyan and she had ridden out there. Lucyan's hands circled her waist lightly as he lifted her onto the gelding, and then he sprang up behind her. Dareena leaned against his strong chest as he reached around her to grip the reins, and lightly inhaled his scent. He smelled of smoke and spice, and she drew in a deeper breath through her nose, the scent oddly addicting.

"You smell good too," Lucyan said, dipping his head. Dareena gasped as his nose grazed the sensitive spot where her neck and shoulder met—that's where Drystan had first sniffed her, too. "Good enough to eat," he added, flicking at the spot with his tongue.

White-hot need lanced straight through Dareena, and she instinctively arched into Lucyan. "I don't think we ought to engage in love play while sitting on a horse," she gasped as Lucyan nibbled her neck. "Someone might get hurt."

Lucyan laughed, lifting his head. "That wasn't love play, darling," he murmured against her ear, and his warm breath sent shivers through her. "That was just a taste of what's to come later."

He spurred the horse into motion before Dareena could answer, and she jolted as the animal began trotting down the hill. "The War of the Three Kingdoms started nearly a thousand years ago," he said in a casual tone, as if just a moment ago he hadn't been grazing his teeth across her exposed flesh. "Back then, my ancestor, King Rakan, had set his sights on Elvenhame. He was a power-hungry bastard, and he coveted the elven lands for their bountiful forests and endless springs. We had many more dragons back then, before the elven goddess cursed us, and Rakan thought he could succeed in his campaign against the elves."

"Why wasn't he able to win?" Dareena asked. "I know the elves are a formidable race"—she knew they were said to have earth magic, and were keen-eyed and fleet-footed— "but I can't see how that compares to dragons and their fire."

"If we'd had to face the elven armies alone, we might have beaten them," Lucyan said. "But the warlocks of Shadowhaven lent their support to Elvenhame because they did not want Dragonfell setting their sights on them next, as would have surely happened if Rakan had taken the elven lands. Warlocks have powerful magic, and with their might joined with Elvenhame's, Dragonfell was forced into a stalemate."

"Oh, right," Dareena said, vaguely remembering this part. "And so they tried to strike a treaty, but King Rakan betrayed them, didn't he?"

"Yes," Lucyan said in a solemn voice. "He slaughtered both the elven and warlock monarchs right where they sat, much to the shock and dismay of his sons. The rest of Dragonfell wanted peace as well—we had lost too many dragons to this war, and it was obvious that we wouldn't win without losing many more. But the sickness of greed had seeped into the dragon king's bones and would not loosen its claws. It had driven King Rakan mad, and he would not listen to reason, not even from his closest advisors."

"That's terrible," Dareena whispered, trying to imagine how the other kingdoms had felt when they'd learned about this horrific loss. "No wonder Shalia cursed our kingdom."

Lucyan stiffened behind her. "The elven goddess's curse was a bit harsh," he said tightly, "particularly since the king's sons were repentant, and immediately subjugated their father and handed him over to the elven lords to be executed. But Shalia's Curse could not be undone." He sighed, and the tension

Dareena felt in him eased a little. "And so here we are, with you torn from your home to serve as the Dragon's Gift, and my brothers and I vying for your favor so that we might continue our noble race."

Dareena twisted a little to look into Lucyan's uncharacteristically solemn face. "Are you saying you wished you didn't have to win me?" she asked. Was it possible that Lucyan didn't want her? A pang hit her heart that she didn't understand—she hadn't fallen for him, and Drystan and Alistair were just as appealing.

Lucyan's trademark grin banished the shadows from his face. "Of course I wish I didn't have to win you," he said. "I want this contest to be over and done with already, so I can take you to bed and plant many dragon babies in your belly."

Dareena's face flamed, and she looked away. Ahead, the Keep loomed close, and within a few moments, they rode through the gates. Lucyan dropped the gelding off at the stables, then took her to the library.

"Well this is no help," Dareena said, sounding disappointed as she leafed through the books that Lucyan brought out for her. "Only two of these books are written in the Common Tongue!"

"Ah, yes." Lucyan looked a little sheepish. "I forgot that you wouldn't be able to read dragon runes. If you'd like, I can teach you. It's merely a matter of learning the alphabet—once you know it, you'll be able to decipher the words easily enough."

Lucyan spent the rest of the afternoon teaching Dareena the alphabet. The runes were complex and hard to draw, but after several hours of drilling with a series of makeshift cards that Lucyan had hastily created with parchment and ink, Dareena was beginning to get the hang of it. Lucyan gave the cards to her to practice on her own, and he insisted she take one of the books back to her room with her so that she might begin deciphering it. The best way to learn how to read, after all, was by reading.

"Thank you," Dareena said when they stopped outside her door. "This has been wonderful."

"The pleasure is all mine," Lucyan said. He moved closer, brushing a lock of raven hair off Dareena's cheek. His touch sent a tiny thrill through her, and she found herself leaning in unconsciously. He brushed his lips against hers once, twice, then gently bit down on her bottom lip in a way that made Dareena hungry for more. She parted her lips, but he drew back just before she could take it further.

"I'm sure you're tired, my lady," he said, bowing his head. "I wouldn't want to exhaust you right before your first day off."

"Oh no you don't," Dareena said, fisting her hand in the collar of his tunic. Lucyan's eyes widened in delight as she pulled him back against her, and they came together in a crash of lips and teeth that should have been awkward, and yet somehow wasn't. The book slipped from Dareena's hand, and a moment later Lucyan gathered her up in his arms and shoved the door open.

"If it's more you want," he growled against her mouth as he set her down on the bed, "I am more than happy to oblige."

Dareena pushed herself up onto her hands as Lucyan kicked off his boots. He crawled across the bed toward her, his eyes glowing with lust, and Dareena's heartbeat kicked up a notch with every breath that he drew closer. By the time he reached her, she was breathing hard, her core pulsing with need. She bunched her skirts in one hand, ready to pull them up so that Lucyan could do, well, whatever it was that men did when they put a hand up a woman's skirts. She didn't know much about lovemaking, but she did know that after two days of unrelieved sexual frustration with Lucyan's brothers, she was going to explode if one of them didn't do something about it soon.

"Ah-ah-ah," Lucyan said in a playful tone, covering his hand with hers before she could pull her skirt up. "That's for me to unwrap, not the other way around."

He covered her body with his own, nudging her skirts up just enough so that he could settle between her legs. His length pressed against her inner thigh as he leaned in to kiss her. She arched her hips, wanting more. But Lucyan only laughed, nudging her legs wider so she couldn't push up off the mattress. He slid his tongue inside her mouth, filling her with his taste and scent, and Dareena groaned as the fire in her lower belly roared even hotter. She reached for him, but he grabbed her hands and pinned them overhead with one hand, forcing her to lie still beneath him. She wanted to curse him, but she had no breath to speak, and a secret part of her actually *liked* that he was dominating her.

Had she gone mad?

She didn't know how long the kiss went on for. It could have been minutes, or it could have been hours. He kissed her long and slow, as if he were doing a thorough but leisurely exploration of her mouth, learning every curve and crevice down to the last detail. He nibbled and licked, sucked and stroked, until Dareena was a trembling mess beneath him, until she couldn't think of anything else *but* him.

"If you think torturing me like this is the way to win me

over," Dareena finally gasped against his mouth, "you might very well find yourself last in the running."

Lucyan chuckled. "There's that fire of yours," he said, nipping at her lower lip. "No wonder the gods chose you to be the Dragon's Gift."

Dareena was about to tell him exactly what he could do with *that* statement when he finally slipped a hand beneath her skirt. She gasped as he cupped her between her legs with his big hand, his long fingers sliding against her damp underthings and sending a bolt of pleasure through her.

"Gods, you're soaked," Lucyan breathed, all levity disappearing from his face. His glowing gaze was intense. "I didn't intend to go this far tonight, but..."

Dareena squealed as he ripped off her underthings in one quick motion. She opened her mouth to protest, but what came out was a throaty groan as his hand finally made contact with her pussy. His long, slightly roughened fingers delved between her slick folds, and her hips came off the bed when his thumb brushed across a particularly sweet spot.

"Found it," Lucyan murmured teasingly. He sank his teeth into her earlobe as he flicked that same spot with his thumb. "Do you like that?"

"Yes," Dareena moaned. "Please, please don't stop." She grabbed his wrist and pressed his hand against her, grinding the heel of his hand exactly where she wanted it.

"Fuck," Lucyan growled, pulling back. For a moment, Dareena thought he was going to remove his hand, but he merely sat up a little, his eyes transfixed on their joined hands.

"Yes," he hissed when she rubbed herself against him. "Show me what you want."

Emboldened, Dareena began to rock her hips against his hand, keeping it pressed against her. Pleasure surged through her with each press of her hips against his palm, and the knot of tension between her legs seemed to tighten with each breath. She was getting close, close to something big...

"That's it," Lucyan panted, rubbing his hand faster against her. "Come for me, darling. You're right there."

Dareena arched her hips one more time, and a hidden dam inside her suddenly burst free. She screamed as wave after wave of pleasure crashed through her, obliterating all other thoughts and sensation. She felt as if she were soaring high above the world and no one could touch her.

"I could make you soar higher and freer than any bird."

The sound of Drystan's voice echoing in her ears was like a bucket of ice water dumped straight over her head. Eyes wide, she bolted upright and nearly smashed her forehead into Lucyan's.

"Dareena?" Lucyan's brow furrowed with concern as he gripped her shoulders. "What's wrong?"

"I..." Dareena panted, pressing a hand against her chest. How could she explain this? "It's nothing," she mumbled, turning away. Her cheeks flamed, and suddenly she wanted to curl up into a ball and hide from Lucyan's too-keen gaze.

"I very much disagree," Lucyan said, his voice soft. Gently, he slid his hand beneath Dareena's jaw and turned her head back to him. "Dareena, please, tell me what happened. Did I do something wrong? Did I hurt you in any way?"

"Hurt me?" Dareena shook her head. "No, Lucyan—you gave me a wonderful experience. And that's the problem."

Lucyan frowned. "I fail to see how bringing you pleasure is a problem," he said quizzically, sitting back on his heels. "Unless the problem is that now you want more?" He waggled his eyebrows.

Dareena laughed despite herself. "Don't be silly," she said, swatting at him. "It's just...I was thinking about Drystan, and the way he makes me feel."

"Ugh." Lucyan twisted his face into an expression of disgust. "Not exactly what a man wants to hear, but I did ask."

Dareena winced. "I wasn't thinking about him while we were...you know." She made a pathetic gesture with her hand. "But right there, at the end, I remembered how much I wanted him while we were together."

Lucyan raised an eyebrow. "Together?"

"No, not like that," Dareena said impatiently. "We came close, but we didn't get as far as you and I did. But the thing is, I *wanted* to. More than anything in the world, at the time. And yet when you touched me tonight...I felt the same thing. How is that possible?"

Lucyan sighed. "While I am probably shooting myself in the foot by admitting it...I don't think it's so strange that you would find my brothers just as sexually enticing. After all, we are related," he added with a wry smile. "I've slept with more women than I care to remember, and while I've had my share of boring lays, I've also had plenty that were spectacular."

"Oh?" Dareena lifted an eyebrow. "And which category do I fall in?"

Lucyan gave her a wicked smile. "Well, I haven't actually lain with you yet"—he leaned in so that his breath ghosted against her lips as he spoke—"but judging by what I've seen so far, I don't think you'll be merely spectacular. I have a feeling you'll be downright *magical*."

Dareena knew he was merely flattering her, and yet she could feel herself swell with pride beneath his praise. "You really know how to make a woman feel special," she teased.

"I aim to please." Lucyan grinned, then pressed a quick kiss against her lips. "As much as I've enjoyed your company, I fear that if I don't take my leave now, I won't come out until morning. I should go now, unless you wish otherwise...?" His voice trailed off hopefully.

Dareena was half tempted to let him stay, to see exactly what else he could do with those talented fingers. He'd made her feel such incredible things, all without taking her clothes off. But the rational part of her knew she needed distance right now to sort through the conflicting experiences.

"As I thought." Lucyan inclined his head, correctly interpreting her hesitation. "Good night, my lady. I hope you'll be thinking of me as you sleep."

He left her with a smile and a wink, and she pondered the day's events as she ate her dinner, then poured over the alphabet cards he'd given her. And while Dareena would think of Lucyan later that night, he would be far from the only dragon prince who waltzed in her dreams.

NINETEEN

Without Dareena to keep him occupied for the day, Drystan decided to do what neither of his brothers ever did: voluntarily spend the day with the king.

He did it for various reasons—first because he believed he'd follow in his footsteps, and seeing what the king did made sense for an heir. But strange as it was, he also did it because he enjoyed it. There, in his office, as they worked together in silence, the king seemed more peaceful than when he was dealing with courtiers or subjects. Less like the volatile dragon he was becoming, and more like the wise, caring father Drystan had grown up with.

Unfortunately, Drystan was getting less of the latter and more of the former as they sat in on another council meeting. This one, as so many of the others, revolved around the ongoing war. All of the councilors had a different opinion, but no one spoke clearly. It was obvious to Drystan that most of the advisors were open to negotiating. The war was so uncertain and controversial, and it brought as much misery to their people as it did to the elves. Not only the men who were killed and wounded, but also the countless widows and fatherless children.

But mentions of the war had a strange effect on the king, forcing the madman to claw to the surface. Drystan could see his personality alter right before his eyes. Why was his father so obsessed with this conflict? He wished Alistair and Lucyan had come with him for this meeting, but Lucyan was off with Dareena, and Alistair had business that apparently couldn't wait. At least Tariana was there, seated opposite him—her sharp features were schooled into an expression of boredom, but Drystan knew his sister saw everything with those keen eyes and was monitoring every person in the room.

"Now may be time to explore all our options, Your Highness," Renflaw, the head of the council, said. He was a thickset, balding man with a bushy white beard, and very well respected at court.

"What is it you're suggesting, my good Renflaw?" the king asked, his tone almost conversational. But Drystan noticed the set of his jaw—he could practically smell the fire building in his father's chest. He held his breath, hoping Renflaw proceeded with caution.

But Renflaw merely set his broad shoulders, ignoring the signs. "It is time to negotiate a peace treaty, my king," he said firmly. "The other councilors and I have discussed it, and—"

"Discussed it?" the king hissed. "You conspire behind my back?"

His lethal gaze swept the room, and the other councilors

shrank back. "We are well within our rights to speak to each other outside of this council room, Your Highness," Renflaw continued doggedly. "Our resources are fast depleting, especially now that no one will trade with us. There are whispers suggesting our enemies are open to negotiating such a treaty."

"He's right, Your Highness," Shadley, the royal spymaster, chimed in as he leaned forward. His thick auburn mustache twitched as he spoke. "I do believe the High King would be amenable to ending this conflict peacefully—"

"So, they are willing to admit defeat?" the king demanded. "Willing to kiss my boot and beg for their miserable lives for murdering my mate?"

Silence descended upon the room. "I don't believe that's quite what they said—" Renflaw began.

"And how is it, exactly," the king said silkily, "that you know what the High King of Elvenhame has been saying? Could it be that you've been consorting with the enemy, Renflaw? Or worse, have you and my spymaster been conspiring against me?"

Renflaw and Shadley turned pale. "My king, we meant no offense—" Shadley began.

"And yet you withhold information like this from me and bring it to the council instead!" the king thundered, banging his fist against the table. The air around him heated by twenty degrees as his eyes blazed red, and the other councilors instinctively leaned away. "You are *my* spymaster, not the other way around! How dare you go behind my back and try to manipulate my council!"

"I'm sorry, my king." Shadley threw himself to the ground near the king's feet. "Please, forgive me."

"I am not in a forgiving mood," the king snarled, throwing back his chair as he got to his feet. Power rolled off him in waves, and Drystan's blood went cold as he jumped to his feet. Was his father going to kill the man right here?

"Darius Shadley, you are hereby charged with conspiring against the crown," the king spat. "You will be held in the dungeons to await trial, and if found guilty, you will be executed for your crimes. Take him away." He gestured to the guards.

"Father!" Tariana rose from her seat, alarm written all over her face. "This is—"

"Do not presume to question me in front of my council," the king spat, turning the might of his fury on Tariana. Drystan's eldest sister stiffened, but she lowered her gaze submissively. Even she, their father's favored, would not dare openly defy him.

"My king! Please!" Shadley cried as the guards grabbed hold of him. He struggled the entire time as they dragged him out of the room before the eyes of the astonished council. "I am a loyal servant! You cannot do this to me!"

The door slammed behind him, the sound echoing in the otherwise dead-silent room. Drystan and Tariana exchanged stricken looks—both of them knew damn well that Shadley was not a traitor. He had been serving the king long before Drystan was born, and Tariana and the spymaster were old friends. But there was nothing they could do, at least not right now. Slowly, the siblings returned to their seats as the king began to prowl, stone-faced, around the table, eyeing each of the councilmen as if they were juicy prey.

"I know there are some amongst you who would sue for

peace at any cost," the king said softly. "I know there are some amongst you who would even go so far as to betray me. But if any of you go behind my back *ever* again, I will see you hang. Is that understood?"

"Yes, my king," the others murmured, sufficiently cowed.

"Good." Satisfied, the king resumed his seat. "Now, where were we?"

Drystan stared at his father. How could he expect that anyone would continue to speak their mind? It was clear that they needed to end the madness that was tearing their land apart, but that madness seemed to have taken root in the king's heart. The only way to be rid of it was to flush it out of him, but Drystan couldn't see how to do that. There was no reasoning with him—anything he or the others might say would be considered treason, and they'd be jailed just as Shadley was.

Poor man. Drystan would have to seek out his siblings after this and see if anything could be done for him.

"Your Highness," Langren, another councilmember, said, "this war must come to an end, I'm sure we all agree. But that doesn't necessarily mean we should consider coming to an agreement with Elvenhame. What of contacting Shadowhaven and formally requesting their assistance? With the warlocks at our sides, we'd crush the elves effortlessly."

Drystan clenched his jaw at the repulsive suggestion. Warlocks were mercenary bastards who dabbled in black magic. He wanted nothing to do with them, but he feared that teaming up with such filth was exactly the kind of thing his father would like.

But to his surprise, the king bared his teeth at the man. "The warlocks have no cause but their own," he snapped. "They're not to be trusted. We will fight as we have always done—using our own might and resources, which are more than enough to crush this elven blight that plagues our world. I don't care how many lives we have to sacrifice—we must win this war."

With that, the king strode from the room. The councilors exchanged uneasy glances, and Drystan was tempted to stay and see what they said. But he knew the men would never talk candidly while he was in the room, so he hurriedly followed his father before the doors slammed shut.

"Fools," his father muttered as Drystan caught up to him. "My council has been reduced to nothing but a bunch of sniveling cowards. I should replace them all!"

Drystan said nothing. He was still wrestling with his own feelings about what had transpired. He'd known all along what was brewing in his father's heart, but to hear him say aloud that he was willing to throw his men's lives away...it was unthinkable. What had happened to the man who had bounced him on his knee and told him stories of the dragons of old when he was a babe? Who had consoled him when he'd accidentally torched the pork roast at dinner when his power had first manifested, and taught him to control his flame?

There must be some way to reason with him, he thought desperately. His father wasn't gone, not completely. The caring man was still buried inside somewhere. He *had* to be.

"Where do you all stand with your Dragon's Gift, my boy?" the king asked abruptly.

Drystan cleared his throat, banishing his anxious train of thought. "It's only been a few days," he said, infusing his voice with confidence, "but I have reason to believe that she favors me."

His father nodded in approval. "And how do you plan to secure her affection? Come, entertain me. I need it after this poor excuse for a council meeting. I can't believe they summoned me for such nonsense."

Because talks of peace are apparently nonsense now, Drystan refrained from saying.

"By being the best," Drystan said simply. "We are taking turns courting the lady, Father, and so far, she is responding very well to my attentions."

The king's booming laughter rang through the Keep's halls. "Court her? That's ridiculous. If it were me, I would have challenged my brothers to a duel, and the last man standing would have won the wench."

"And I would have, if my competitors hadn't also been my brothers," Drystan said calmly, even as his hackles rose at the way his father had called Dareena "wench." As if she were a servant, or a whore. "You're the one who set the terms, Father. She's to choose, so we are simply giving her an opportunity to make up her mind."

The king rolled his eyes. "This is why I have a hard time believing any of you are worthy of wearing the crown. This commoner is nothing but a trophy and a broodmare. You should not elevate her to an importance beyond her station."

Before Drystan could respond, Dareena rounded the corner and nearly ran into both men. "Your Highnesses," she said quickly, dipping into a curtsy. Her eyes were lowered to the ground, but Drystan caught the flash of hurt in them. Had she heard what his father had said?

"My lady," Drystan said, inclining his head in return. He wished that she would look up at him so he could attempt to convey how sorry he was for his father's harsh words, but instead she moved past them both and continued down the long, decorated hall, her shoulders stiff and her spine ramrod straight.

Damn. He would have to apologize later.

"Well, well," his father said as she vanished from sight, "it seems that she will make a fine wife after all. The wench certainly knows how to look pretty and stay out of business. Let's hope she remembers how to do so when one of you finally becomes king."

TWENTY

"What an ass," Dareena fumed as she paced back and forth in her room. Tears of humiliation and anger stung her eyes—she could still see the look on the king's face when she'd run into him and Drystan in the hall, as if she were nothing but a piece of meat. She'd been coming back from the kitchens after grabbing a bite to eat, and now she desperately wished she'd never left her room.

A trophy and a broodmare, the king had called her.

And so what if he did? a nasty voice in her head sneered. *Isn't that exactly what you would have been as the innkeeper's wife? How is this any different?*

Dareena clenched her jaw. The only difference between being Mr. Harrin's wife and the Dragon's Gift was that she got to wear fancier dresses and sleep in a feather bed. In the end, she existed only to serve the pleasure of her husband—her own needs and desires came second.

She might have a choice in which of the princes was to *be*

that husband, but the cage remained the same. What did it matter which one she chose? She might as well draw straws, just as the princes had when they'd been squabbling over which one would take her out first. Wasn't this all just a game, in the end? For all of them?

A knock on the door interrupted her pity party. "Dareena?" Drystan called. "Are you in there?"

"It's my day off, Drystan," she called back angrily. "Leave me alone."

There was a long pause. "I didn't come to harass you," Drystan said. "I came to apologize."

The pain in his voice melted some of Dareena's anger, and she crossed the room to let him in. His face was grave as he shut the door behind him, then gently took her into his arms.

"You've been crying," he said quietly, tracing the tear track on her cheek with his thumb. "I'm sorry. I didn't mean for you to get hurt."

"I know you didn't." Dareena turned away from his tender gaze—she couldn't bear to look at him right now. "It's just...you let your father talk about me as if I were a piece of trash."

"Let?" Drystan let out a harsh laugh. "Dareena, one doesn't 'let' the king do anything. He does what he likes, and crushes anyone who attempts to stand in his way. Let him have his petty words. They don't matter. You know that I don't think you're just a trophy. None of us do."

"I know." Dareena turned back to Drystan and laid a hand on his cheek. His beard prickled against her palm, a rough but pleasant sensation. "It's just...this is frustrating for me. I like all three of you. How am I supposed to choose? I know we still have two more weeks...but that just doesn't seem like enough time."

"It's all we have," Drystan said softly. He ran a hand gently over Dareena's hair, then tucked a lock behind her ear. "I know that Lucyan tried to pass off Father's comment about marrying you as a joke...but I'm not entirely sure he wouldn't, if you didn't choose one of us."

Dareena recoiled in horror. "He couldn't possibly. That's sacrilegious, isn't it?"

Drystan's lips twisted into a mockery of a smile. "There isn't anything specifically forbidding it," he said. "Which is what I'm sure my father would say if anyone protested. I would like to think he wouldn't do such a thing, but these past few years...he hasn't been himself, Dareena. Not since Mother died."

"Oh." Dareena's indignation faded a bit at the sadness she glimpsed in Drystan's eyes. "That must have been very hard on you."

"It was hard on all of us," Drystan said tightly. "But hard on Father the most. He believes the elves are responsible for Mother's death."

"Is that why we are at war?"

Drystan sighed. "There are many reasons one goes to war."

"That's not an answer."

Drystan scraped a hand over his beard. "I don't have any answers for you, Dareena. Not where my father is concerned. Someday, I will be strong enough to challenge him, but until that day comes, we must all bend the knee. There is no telling what my father will do if any one of us defies him—his moods are as capricious as the wind. You saw him that day in the audience chamber—he indulged Alistair and Lucyan in their proposal to allow you to choose, but he could just as well have swung the other way. Every time we challenge or negotiate with him, we're taking a great risk."

Dareena nodded. "I understand," she said, and she really did. Drystan and his brothers weren't happy with the king, but until they knew they had a chance at winning, they could not openly challenge his rule. For Drystan to tell her this, when just talking about overthrowing the king was tantamount to treason...

"Thank you," she said, taking his hand in hers, "for trusting me enough to tell me the truth."

Drystan smiled, then raised her hand so he could kiss her knuckles. The sensation of his warm lips on her skin sent a tiny shiver through her. "I should go now," he said. "I'll see you tomorrow."

"Wait." Dareena grabbed his wrist as he turned away. "Don't go. Stay with me awhile."

Drystan frowned. "I'm not sure that's a good idea. If my brothers found out that I spent time with you when it isn't my day, they would flay me alive."

"My evenings are still my own," Dareena said firmly, pulling him closer. "If I wish to spend this one with one of you, that is my prerogative."

Drystan laughed. "Very well," he said, circling Dareena's waist with his big hands. "And how exactly do you wish to spend the rest of this evening?"

Dareena's eyes twinkled. "The way I spend most evenings," she said, wrapping her arms around his neck. "In bed."

She kissed Drystan deeply, and he growled against her

mouth as he scooped her up, happy to oblige. Lips fused, he carried her to the bed, and they fell on the mattress together, hands roaming over each other's bodies. Drystan found the ties to Dareena's bodice and managed to make short work of it—he yanked her dress until it was down around her hips, baring her breasts to his glowing amber eyes.

"Oh, yes," he said, rearing back so that he could gaze at her half-naked form. He cupped one of her breasts in his left hand. "You have beautiful breasts. I can't tell you how many times I've fantasized about finally seeing them."

Dareena blushed beneath his intense regard. He scraped the pad of his thumb across her nipple, and she moaned, arching into his touch. "Sensitive, too," he murmured, cupping the other breast. "All the better for me."

"What are you—" Dareena began to ask as he dipped his head down, then she moaned when he flicked his tongue over her other nipple. The sensation made her pussy clench with need, and she squirmed beneath him when he did it again. She slid her hands into his dark hair as he feasted on one breast while massaging the other, holding him close so that he wouldn't stop. She had no idea that playing with her breasts could feel so good—she had always thought they were just for feeding babies, and for men to look at.

And why wouldn't they be for your pleasure too? They're part of your body, aren't they?

"Drystan," Dareena moaned when she finally couldn't take it anymore. "Please..." She grabbed the hand on her breast and guided it between her legs. "Touch me here."

"A woman who knows what she wants." Drystan lifted his

head, his handsome face alight with a pleased grin. "I like that. But I can do much better, my lady."

He pulled the rest of her dress off, along with her underwear, leaving her completely naked. Dareena expected him to cup her between her legs, as Lucyan had done, but instead he lowered his mouth to her breast, then began to kiss and lick a path down her belly. Each touch and caress of his lips and tongue sent little thrills of pleasure through Dareena, heightening the anticipation. She watched through hooded eyes as Drystan nibbled on the skin just above her hip bones, then nudged her legs wider.

"What are you doing?" Dareena asked as he hooked her knees over his powerful shoulders. It was strange to see him kneeling before her naked body while he was fully clothed. Shouldn't he be naked as well?

"This," Drystan said, leaning in. He dragged his hot tongue across her wet folds, and Dareena cried out, hips arching into his mouth. Drystan slid his hands beneath her bottom, his strong fingers digging into the rounded globes of her ass as he licked and sucked at her pussy in earnest. His skilled tongue quickly found her sweet spot, and the next thing she knew she was flying, just like she had when she'd pressed Lucyan's hand between her legs.

Except this time, she did not merely fly once. Dareena thought he would put her down after this, but he kept on licking until another tsunami of pleasure crashed down on her, and another. She was certain the entire castle could hear as she moaned Drystan's name out loud, over and over again, but she didn't give a damn. All she cared about was the way he made her feel. As if, at this very moment, they were the only two people in the world, standing together in the eye of a wonderful storm that she hoped would never end.

"I love the way you say my name," Drystan panted when he finally lifted his head. His mouth and beard glistened as he looked at her with those glowing eyes—it was one of the sexiest things Dareena had ever seen. "I want you to say it again, with my cock buried deep inside you."

"Yes." Dareena reached for him. "Take off your clothes," she demanded, tugging on his tunic belt.

She sat back to watch as Drystan stripped for her, revealing the big, muscular body she'd fantasized about on more than one occasion. His physique was even more defined than she'd thought, his arms and legs thick with corded muscle, and his broad chest and abs were covered with a fine dusting of black hair.

But it was his cock that truly held her attention, long and thick, with a glistening head that seemed to beg for her attention. Transfixed, Dareena reached for it, wrapping her fingers around his girth. Drystan groaned a little as she glided her fingers up and down, familiarizing herself with it. She'd seen cocks before but had never had the chance to touch one until now.

"It's hard and soft at the same time," she murmured, sliding her thumb over the tip, which was wet. "Like a sword wrapped in silk."

Drystan choked out a laugh. "That's one way to put it." He gently pulled her hand away. "I don't want you to play with it too much," he said when she began to protest. "At least not yet."

Dareena let him guide her back down to the bed. Her heart beat faster as he nudged her legs apart, then took his cock into his hand and gently rubbed the tip against her folds. "So wet," he murmured, his gaze transfixed as he coated himself in her juices. "You're ready, aren't you?"

Dareena nodded. She had thought she might feel guilty, as she had with Lucyan the other night, but the truth was, she needed to do this. The sexual tension she felt when she was with the brothers was clouding her judgment and making it too hard to choose between them. Having sex with all three of them would help get that out of the way so she could focus on what really mattered—their personalities.

"This might be a little uncomfortable for you at first," Drystan warned. "But I'm going to try and get you past that as quickly as I can. Do you trust me?"

"Yes," Dareena breathed. She watched as Drystan pressed the tip of his cock against her sweet spot, and she instinctively arched into him, rubbing herself against his hard length. He rocked his hips forward a little, creating more friction, and Dareena moaned, feeling herself get even wetter. Her pussy ached with the need to have him fill her, to bring her the sweet relief she'd been craving since the day he'd kissed her in the carriage.

"Yes," he growled, pulling back as she rocked her hips in earnest. "You're ready."

He surged into her without warning, breaking her hymen in one swift, decisive stroke. Dareena cried out as she felt something give inside her with a quick flash of pain. She dug her fingers into Drystan's shoulders and held on tight as he filled her to the brim.

"Shhh." Drystan held his hips very still as he reached between them. "It will get better in a moment. I promise."

His fingers quickly found her sweet spot again, and he stroked her gently, making her forget all about the brief pain as pleasure filled her again. After a few moments, Dareena arched her hips into his hand, and they both groaned as Drystan slid even deeper inside her.

"You're so tight," he gasped, his forehead pressed against hers. "So tight and wet. It's incredible." He pulled out a little, then gently sank back in.

"Yes," Dareena moaned, sliding her hands down his back so she could grip his muscled ass. "More." She rocked her hips, back and forth, back and forth, reveling in the feeling of his cock sliding in and out of her. The way he stretched and filled her was both satisfying and maddening, each stroke bringing her closer to fulfillment, and yet not nearly close enough.

"Come for me," he growled, quickening his strokes. "You're close. I can feel your pussy getting tighter." He kissed her deeply, thrusting hard, and Dareena screamed into his mouth as she tumbled headlong into the most intense orgasm she'd ever experienced.

"*Yes*," Drystan howled triumphantly. He fucked her harder, faster, heightening her orgasm and then sending her straight into another one. All Dareena could do was hold on for dear life as he rode her, the bed shaking beneath them as he pounded into her. His face was taut with strain, teeth bared, tanned skin glistening in the lamplight. Instinct drove her to wrap her legs around his waist, and she squeezed hard with her inner walls, driving him over the edge.

"*Dareena,*" he roared as his hot seed gushed inside her. Dareena watched in awe as his big body trembled, as his features grew even more taut and then finally relaxed into the most blissful expression she'd ever seen. He collapsed, then immediately rolled onto his side, gathering her into his arms.

"Wow." She pressed her ear to his damp chest, listening to his thundering heartbeat. A deep satisfaction swept through her, and suddenly she felt languorous. "That was incredible."

"*You* were incredible," he said, pressing a kiss to the top of her head. She snuggled in tight against him, and as they both drifted off to sleep, she wondered if any of the other brothers could possibly top this.

TWENTY-ONE

When Drystan left Dareena's rooms later that night, he felt as if he were flying. He'd actually done it! He'd been the first of his brothers to make love to the Dragon's Gift. Pride surged through him as he remembered how she'd moaned with pleasure, scoring his back with her sharp little nails as she came. What a delightful vixen she was. He was certain that she would be coming back for more, and that at the end of the three weeks, his father would proclaim him heir.

Part of him wanted to shake his brothers awake and crow to the rooftops about what he'd accomplished, but Drystan wasn't childish enough to give in to such an urge. Besides, his brothers would take the news better if they had some sleep first. But as Drystan was passing Alistair's rooms on the way to his own, he heard voices coming from beneath his brother's door.

"I can't believe Father did this," Lucyan muttered, and Drystan frowned. Lucyan rarely visited Alistair in his quarters, especially not late at night. What was going on? "He truly is going mad."

"Are you certain he's going to prosecute?" Alistair asked. "That he isn't just throwing Shadley into the dungeons to teach him a lesson?"

"I saw the look in Father's eyes." That was Tariana, her voice as grim as Drystan's mood was becoming. The afterglow dropped away as he remembered the council meeting—Dareena's sweet curves and luscious mouth had made him forget poor Shadley's predicament. "He means to kill the spymaster."

Drystan pushed the door open. "She's right," he announced as the others turned to him with surprise. "And we cannot simply stand by and let it happen. We must do something to help Shadley."

"Break the rules, brother?" Lucyan arched an eyebrow. "I never thought the day would come when you would openly defy Father."

Drystan dropped into one of Alistair's chairs, right next to his youngest brother. "Desperate times require desperate measures," he said with a sigh. "Shadley has done nothing wrong—we cannot let him go to the gallows."

"We will have to resc—" Alistair cut himself off, his eyes narrowing. He leaned toward Drystan, his nostrils flaring as he drew in a deep breath. "You..." His face slacked. "You smell like sex."

Lucyan's eyes grew wide, and he leaned in for a sniff as well. "Damn," he cursed, recoiling as if he smelled something repulsive. "You've had sex with Dareena, haven't you?"

Drystan cringed inwardly—this wasn't exactly how he wanted this conversation to go. "I don't think that's especially relevant right now—"

"Of course it is." Alistair jumped to his feet. "You've given Dareena her first sexual experience. She's bound to choose you."

Lucyan snorted. "Don't be ridiculous. The three weeks aren't up yet, and besides, Drystan wasn't the first. I gave our sweet little minx her fair share of orgasms the other day."

It was Drystan's turn to look surprised. "Did you? She never mentioned that to me."

Lucyan laughed. "Yes, I'm sure she thought that was a fantastic idea while your hands were up her skirts. Lucky for you she wasn't screaming my name when you made her come, or you would have a real problem, wouldn't you?"

Drystan set his jaw. "You're a real prick sometimes—"

"Enough!" Tariana snapped. "While the three of you are bickering about Dareena's magic pussy, Shadley is rotting away in the dungeons beneath our feet. I need to check in with my captains in the morning, so I don't have the luxury of time like you three. If we are going to rescue him, it must happen tonight."

The brothers exchanged glances. "Very well," Drystan said. "Does anyone have suggestions as to how to go about this? We might be royalty, but it isn't as if we can just waltz right in and take Shadley out from beneath the guards' noses."

"Actually," Lucyan said, a slow smile spreading across his face, "I have a plan that might enable us to do exactly that."

FORTY MINUTES LATER, Drystan was grumbling silently to himself as he crawled through a ventilation tunnel beneath the castle floor. This filthy passageway, if one could call it that, had likely never been cleaned, and he was getting all manner of muck on his clothing. It was a good thing that he'd changed into old clothing for this, but he imagined it would take a week of scrubbing to get all the filth out of his hair and skin when he was through. Why was it that when he drew straws against Lucyan, he *always* lost? The bastard was cheating somehow, and one day Drystan would catch him in the act.

Still, he could deal with a bit of dirt if it meant saving Shadley's life. If this was the worst thing Drystan had to complain about in his life, then he was damn lucky.

Drystan did his best to be quiet as he crawled on his hands and knees through the tunnel, but still, his rough clothes scraped against the old stone as he moved. He held his breath as he passed by each of the cells, praying to the dragon god that no prisoner or guard was close enough to hear. Thankfully most of the cells were empty, and the guards were not patrolling the dungeon—they were likely in the guardroom, playing cards and trading stories while one of them stood posted outside the dungeon door.

After what seemed like an eternity, Drystan reached Shadley's cell. The spymaster was lying on his hard cot, staring listlessly at the ceiling. Drystan felt a twinge of sympathy as he stared down at the man through the grate. He was a loyal servant to the crown—he didn't deserve to be caged like an animal.

"Shadley," he hissed, pressing his face as close to the ventilation grate as he dared.

The spymaster bolted upright, looking around. "Who's there?" he asked in a hushed voice, his gaze darting about.

"Up here!" Drystan stuck his fingers through the grate and waggled them. Shadley's eyes widened as he finally looked up at the grate, and he climbed up onto his cot so he could peer inside.

"Prince Drystan?" he whispered, astonished. "What are you doing here?"

"Rescuing you." Drystan fished out Lucyan's ratty invisibility cloak, which he'd stuffed down his shirt. He slipped it to Shadley through the grate. "This cloak will make you invisible for a short period of time. Put it on the next time you hear someone approach, and don't make *any* sound. As soon as the opportunity presents itself, head straight for the Dustman's Bluff. Help will be waiting for you there."

"But how—"

"No more talking!" Drystan hissed. "Just get down and follow my orders."

Shadley nodded, then climbed down and lay down on the cot. Drystan pulled his face back from the grate just enough to ensure nobody could see him, then settled in to wait.

A few minutes later, the door at the end of the hall opened. Shadley quickly put the cloak on as footsteps rasped against the stone floor, and he disappeared from view just as Lucyan and Alistair showed up with a pair of guards.

"What is the meaning of this?" Alistair demanded, rounding on the guards. "I thought you said the prisoner was here!"

"He is!" The guard's eyes darted nervously toward the cell.

"Or at least, he was. I don't understand how he could have gotten out."

"The gate is still shut," the second guard said, examining the lock. "Doesn't look like it's been tampered with."

"What are you, some kind of simpleton?" Lucyan scoffed. "The man is a spymaster. He can break in and out of buildings without leaving a trace behind. He must have smuggled his lock picks in with him."

"That's impossible," the first guard protested. "We searched him thoroughly."

"Not thoroughly enough," Alistair said grimly. "Open up the cell. He may have left something inside that will help us figure out where he's gone."

The guards exchanged dubious glances but did as Alistair asked. No doubt they feared what would happen if they objected, considering that they'd already "lost" the prisoner. "We'll have to alert the king," the second guard said in a worried voice as he opened the cell.

"I'll go first," Alistair commanded, nudging the guard aside. He opened the cell door wide. "Men like Shadley are tricky. He may have left behind a trap."

"All the better for me to go first, my prince," the guard protested, but Alistair ignored him. He shifted his body subtly, making a space just wide enough for Shadley to slip past, and paused for a few seconds before entering the cell. His gaze met Drystan's through the grate, and he nodded with a barely discernable dip of his chin.

Satisfied, Drystan crawled the rest of the way through the ventilation tunnel, his brothers making sufficient noise that the guards wouldn't hear him. He emerged at the other end into a closet that led out to one of the servant passages. Dusting himself off as best he could, he glanced to see if anyone was nearby, then quietly made his way back to his quarters. Part of him wanted to follow Shadley out to the docks and make sure he got there safely, but there was no way to do it without alerting the guard of his departure, and he couldn't risk that.

No, at this point, Shadley's life was in Tariana's hands. She was waiting for him with supplies and would carry him to safety on her way to the front lines. Lucyan and Alistair would lead the search party to ensure that the guards didn't catch up with Shadley. With nothing more to do except fret, Drystan returned to his rooms to wash off the evidence of his crime and pray that his father never learned the truth about what they had done tonight.

TWENTY-TWO

The next morning, Alistair and Lucyan were summoned to the king's chambers.

They stood in silence as the king sat at his breakfast table, watching him as he tore into a quail. The bird's juices dripped down his chin and fingers as he devoured the animal, tearing strips of meat off the bones before he broke them in half and sucked out the marrow. There was an array of food spread on the table as well—potatoes, vegetables, and a bowl of fresh fruit.

It took everything Alistair had to hold his tongue.

He knew damn well why the king had dragged them here after they'd both spent a sleepless night thinking about what they'd done, worrying if Shadley had made it to Dustman's Bluff and if Tariana had carried him to safety. There was no way to know until she returned—she would not risk sending a message by parchment, even a coded one. They would just have to deal with the agonizing suspense in the meantime.

Alistair risked a glance toward Lucyan, who stood next to him. His brother looked relaxed, almost bored, but Alistair knew that beneath his lackadaisical manner his brother was just as nervous as he. Was it possible their father had found out what they had done? Had he already recaptured Shadley and made the spymaster sing the details of his escape?

"My guards reported something interesting to me last night," the king said, finally breaking the silence.

"Oh?" Lucyan asked, sounding just as bored as he looked. "Have they captured an elven spy? Someone we can interrogate?"

Their father wiped his fingers with a napkin. "Don't play games with me, Lucyan," he said, his voice deceptively calm. "You and Alistair paid a visit to my ex-spymaster last night. Without asking my leave first."

"We weren't aware that we needed your permission to question prisoners, Father," Alistair said blandly. "Lucyan and I weren't at the council meeting when you had him jailed, so we missed the excitement. I thought we might be proactive and turn the screws on him to see what other machinations he might be up to."

"Your initiative would be commendable," the king said, "if you had actually done such a thing. And yet, somehow, when the two of you arrived to question the prisoner, he was already gone from his cell."

There was a beat of silence. "Are you going to give us permission to widen the search, then?" Lucyan asked. "We scoured the entire city and surrounding areas looking for Shadley last night, but—"

"Without informing me that you intended to do that, either." The king's voice heated with anger. "Did I give either of you leave to mount horses and go riding off in the middle of the night? I made it very clear that none of you were to leave the city before I have proclaimed an heir!"

"Do you expect us to stand by and do nothing while our country is at war?" Alistair demanded, finally giving rein to some of his anger. "You trained us to be leaders, Father, not to sit on our hands like ninnies. We saw an opportunity to be useful, and we took it!"

"Useful?" the king repeated. "No. What you saw was an opportunity to defy me." He rose from his chair, the air around him heating with power. Goosebumps raced across Alistair's skin as their father's eyes blazed red. "One of you may become king someday, but as of right now, it is still I, King Dragomir, who sits on Dragonfell's throne. The next time either one of you forgets that, I will have you whipped and chained in the dungeons for a month. Is that clear?"

"Yes, Father," Alistair and Lucyan said as one. Like Alistair, Lucyan's voice was full of barely leashed anger, but both brothers bowed their heads submissively. There was no need to push their father, not when they were getting away free and clear. Their father might suspect, but he had no proof, and even he could not charge them with crimes based on mere suppositions.

One of the few perks of being their father's sons.

"Good. Now get out and let me enjoy the rest of my meal in peace."

"That was a close one," Lucyan muttered once they were far

down the hall, well out of earshot. "I sincerely hope Father doesn't commit any more wrongful arrests. I'm not sure we'd survive another rescue attempt."

"You're not kidding," Alistair said under his breath. The two parted ways at the end of the hall, Lucyan headed off to some appointment, while Alistair went back to his rooms to freshen up. He was supposed to take Dareena out today, but after last night, he wasn't sure there was any point. Drystan had already slept with her, and Lucyan had come damn close. All Alistair had managed was a kiss. How had he convinced himself he'd ever had a chance with Dareena?

Weary, he pushed open the door to his bedroom, intending on a short nap before he went to visit Dareena. But before he could so much as shuck off his boots, he stopped short as a familiar figure slowly sat up from his bed.

"Hi, Alistair," Dareena said shyly. She was covered in nothing but a sheet and the long, unbound black hair cascading around her graceful shoulders. A bare calf peeked out from beneath the covering, and dainty toes gently touched the floor. "I thought I'd surprise you."

"I..." Alistair's mouth went dry as Dareena stood up. The sheet slid away from her body, baring her luscious curves to his wide-eyed gaze. Stunned, he took in all her naked glory, his cock instantly growing hard. Her breasts were large and perky, and his hands itched to squeeze them, to roll those dusky rose nipples beneath his thumbs and make her moan with pleasure. Her small waist flared into wide hips, which in turn flowed gracefully into long, beautifully shaped legs. And between the apex of her thighs was a patch of dark curls he ached to dive into...

"Well?" She lifted an eyebrow. "Are you just going to stare all day?"

"No, it's just..." Alistair swallowed hard. "I thought you'd be warming Drystan's bed."

Dareena moved closer. "And why would I be doing that?" she asked, twining her arms around his neck. She pressed her bare breasts against his chest as she did so, sending a jolt of heat straight to his groin. "This is our day together, isn't it?"

"Yes, but..." Alistair groaned when she rose up on her tippy toes and nipped at his bottom lip. "I thought you didn't want me. You've had Drystan and Lucyan in your bed, but we..."

"Have not," Dareena finished. "And that is exactly what I am trying to remedy. Now are you going to kiss me, or do you plan on talking me to death instead?"

Alistair growled, the dragon in him responding at the challenge in Dareena's voice. He crushed his mouth against hers, kissing her deeply as he wrapped his arms tightly around her. If she'd come here wanting a good fuck, that's what he'd give her, Drystan and Lucyan be damned. He'd make her scream to the rooftops with pleasure until the only name she remembered was his.

Dareena kissed him back just as fiercely, her mouth opening eagerly for him when he bit down on her lower lip. Their tongues met in a clash of raw need, and Alistair devoured her as though he were a starving man and she a juicy peach. Her addictive scent filled his nose, drugging him to the point where all he could think about was getting inside her, and his rough hands roamed over her body, savoring the feel of her smooth skin. She arched into his touch as her hands found the belt of his tunic and tugged, and the next thing he knew his trousers were around his knees.

"Yes," he gasped when she wrapped her dainty fingers around his cock. She stroked him, hesitantly at first, but then grew bolder, her fist moving up and down his aching shaft effortlessly. Her touch was divine, and he could have let her go on like that all night if he didn't have bigger plans for her.

"Enough," he panted, pulling her hand away. He sank to his knees as he kissed a path down the center of her body, stopping to taste her nipples and dip his tongue into her navel. She gasped with each nip and lick, writhing beneath him, and he gripped her hips to keep her steady when he finally reached the patch of curls between her legs. Her thighs opened readily for him, sliding up over his shoulders as he buried his face between her legs and licked her already sopping-wet folds.

"Alistair," she cried, burying a hand in his hair. Gods, the sound of his name on her lips was nearly enough to make him come. She arched her hips into his face as he feasted on her, finding her sweet spot easily. He teased it mercilessly with his tongue, alternating between lazy circles and hard flicks, until her thighs clamped hard around his head and her entire body trembled as she came.

And then he did it again, and again, and again.

"Please," Dareena finally begged, attempting to push him away. "I can't take any more."

"Oh, I'm afraid we're just getting started." Alistair lifted his head, a grin spreading across his face. He lifted her onto the bed and kissed her again, letting her taste herself all over his tongue. When her hands slid down, reaching for his cock again, he gently removed them, then pinned both of them over her head with one hand.

"Don't be in such a hurry," he teased, nipping at her lower lip again. "I want to take my time with you."

"If you take any longer," Dareena said through gritted teeth as she strained against him, "I might end up going mad."

Alistair laughed. He nudged her legs apart, then slowly pushed inside her. Dareena moaned, lifting her hips to take him in deeper, but he used his other hand to hold her steady as he slid into her, savoring her inch by glorious inch. Her pussy was incredible, so hot and tight and wet, and he groaned aloud as he finally buried himself to the hilt.

At first, he moved inside her with gentle strokes, soft and easy. Dareena smiled as she stared up at him, her emerald eyes glowing with passion, and she gently traced the planes of his face. Alistair felt a swell of emotion in his chest, and he leaned down to kiss her again, thrusting harder. How had he grown to feel so much for this woman so fast? He should have been repelled by the fact that Drystan had just been inside her the other day, and yet that didn't bother him as much as he'd thought. It only spurred him on, urging him to do better, to fuck her harder and deeper until her mind and body were drenched in pleasure.

"Ooh," Dareena moaned as she clung to him. The bed shook beneath them as he pounded into her relentlessly, hunger clawing at him, demanding to take what was his. He released her wrists, then guided one of her hands between her legs, urging her to stroke herself. Her eyes glazed over as she did so, and within seconds, she was screaming his name again, her inner muscles clenching around his cock.

"Yes," he groaned as he finally came. He shook with the force of it, gripping the top of the headboard so he wouldn't collapse on top of Dareena. She gently stroked the backs of his legs as he clung there for a long minute, gasping for breath as the world slowly came back into focus around him.

"That was..." He trailed off, shaking his head as he looked at her.

"Amazing?" She smiled, then gently pulled him back down onto the bed with her. Alistair felt another surge of emotion as she snuggled against his chest, and he wrapped his arms around her possessively. A few strands of her black hair tickled his nose, but he didn't mind. He loved the feel of her in his arms, far more than any woman he'd slept with before this. How could he possibly give this up? He had to win her. The alternative was just unthinkable.

"I know you're likely confused," Dareena said after several peaceful moments had passed. She looked up at him through hooded eyes. "You thought that because I let Drystan take my virginity, I chose him."

"Well, that is the general presumption." Alistair gently pushed aside a strand of hair that clung to her cheek. "But I imagine that is not the case, since you're in bed with me now."

"You imagine correctly," she said, pressing a soft kiss against his lips. "You have to understand...just a few weeks ago, my only marriage prospect was an old man. Now, I have three young, virile, handsome dragons to choose from. If I am to make the right choice, I have to get to know all three of you, in every sense of the word."

"In and out of the bedroom, you mean." Alistair should have found the notion offensive, but instead, he chuckled. "You're an oddly practical thing, you know."

Dareena smiled. "I'm not sure if that's meant to be an insult or a compliment."

"I would never insult you, my lady." Alistair reached between their bodies, then slid two fingers inside her. She arched against his hand, and a thrill went through him—she was still wet, still ready. "I think far too much of you for that."

"What are you doing?" she gasped as he began to thrust his fingers into her. Her head fell back against the pillow, and Alistair grinned—those gorgeous eyes were already beginning to glaze over.

"Helping you get to know me," he said suggestively. He leaned in to nip at her ear, and added, "Unless you have a better idea as to how you'd like to spend the rest of the afternoon?"

A breathy moan was his only answer.

TWENTY-THREE

Drystan panted as he weaved left, narrowly dodging Alistair's well-timed punch. He was barely able to keep up with his younger brother as the two of them practiced in the sparring room, as they always did during their weekly training ritual. The jabs were coming in hard and fast, and Drystan had already taken two hits to the ribs and a glancing blow off his temple.

Of course, it wasn't abnormal for Alistair's punches to connect. He *was* the superior fighter. But they were barely two minutes into the fight, and Drystan already felt like they'd gone five rounds. Sweat poured off his forehead, stinging his eyes, and his shirt clung to his body. An inferno raged inside him, and while normally heat didn't bother him, today he felt as if he were going to faint.

"Are you all right?" Alistair asked, his eyebrows furrowed in concern. He dodged a swing from Drystan easily, then pivoted so that he was behind his brother. "You're losing worse than usual."

"Shut up," Drystan growled. He didn't know why, but his arms and legs felt heavy, as if moving through water. He spun on his heel and tried to backfist Alistair, but his brother ducked, then slammed his fist into Drystan's cheek. Drystan stumbled back, stars in his eyes as pain radiated from his cheekbone. White-hot anger surged through him, and he swung again, putting every ounce of strength into the punch. His fist connected with Alistair's jaw with a crack, and his brother went flying across the room.

"Alistair!" Drystan cried as his brother slammed into the wall, then slumped to the ground like a rag doll. The anger disappeared completely, leaving only horror behind as Drystan rushed forward to where his brother lay unconscious. "Brother, are you all right?" He grabbed Alistair's shoulders and shook them. His blond head lolled, and for a moment, Drystan was terrified he'd gone too far.

But then his youngest brother let out a groan, his amber eyes fluttering open. "What in blue blazes was that?" he moaned, tilting his head back to look up at Drystan.

"Thank the gods." Drystan clasped his hands hard as relief coursed through him. "I...I'm sorry, brother. I have no idea what came over me."

"That was some punch," Alistair said. His eyes narrowed suspiciously as he studied Drystan's face. "I can't remember the last time you knocked me out, never mind sending me flying across the room. And just moments ago you looked like you were about to keel over. What's going on?"

"I...I don't know." Drystan pressed a hand to his head. His temple was throbbing, and now that the adrenaline rush was over, his limbs were heavy again, like they were weighed down with wet sand. What was happening to him? There weren't many illnesses dragons could be affected by, and none of them were natural. Had he been poisoned?

"Let's call a healer," Alistair suggested, and Drystan nodded. In their family, they knew better than to ignore strange symptoms. Their mother had suffered from something strange and unexplainable, but she'd brushed it off. They all knew how that had ended.

Drystan stumbled to the door, then called for a servant to fetch the healer. A few minutes later, a white-robed man arrived, a medical pouch on his hips as well as a basket of supplies on his arm. The healer examined them both, frowning, but found nothing.

"What exactly happened?" he finally asked.

"I'm not sure," Drystan said. "I was sparring with Alistair, and I just felt so heavy, so tired. I could barely keep my arms up. Then all of a sudden, I felt this surge of anger and energy, and when I punched him..."

Words failed him, and he gestured lamely to the damaged wall. He couldn't figure out how to explain this. It made no sense at all.

"I don't think there's anything wrong with either of you," said the healer. "You seem quite healthy." Then, he cleared his throat and awkwardly added, "Pardon me for mentioning it, but there's now a Dragon's Gift under your roof..."

Drystan cocked a brow, wondering why the healer seemed so reluctant to finish.

"There is," Alistair said. "What does that have to do with my brother's behavior?"

"Well." The healer cleared his throat. "Everyone knows that the Dragon's Gift makes her king more powerful when they mate. If either of you had, by chance..." He trailed off, his cheeks turning pink.

Drystan and Alistair exchanged alarmed glances. "We get the point," Drystan said, sparing the man from further embarrassment.

The healer nodded, looking relieved. "The sweat, the pendulum swings between weakness and surges of strength—well, I've not been at leisure to study many of you, as I wasn't yet a healer when our king was a young dragon, but I believe King Dragomir experienced similar symptoms when he finally matured."

The brothers froze. "You...you're not referring to the Change, are you?" Alistair asked.

Drystan stared down at his hands. Could he really be this close to shifting? Even now, he could still feel that inferno blazing beneath his skin, uncomfortably hot. Usually he could call his flames forth and dispel them at will, but he couldn't seem to get rid of this blasted heat no matter how hard he tried to focus.

"There has to be another explanation," he finally said. Male dragons didn't mature until they hit their fiftieth year, and they were barely thirty.

"Of course, my prince," he said smoothly. "Perhaps you've simply overtaxed yourself and need more rest."

Alistair and Drystan exchanged uneasy glances as the healer went about mixing up some concoctions from his pouches of herbs. He handed Alistair a bottle of bright blue liquid. "For the pain in your ribs," he told him—he'd determined in his examination that Alistair had cracked two of them when he'd slammed into the wall. "You'll heal on your own, of course, but this should speed up the process. And this," he said, handing Drystan a green bottle, "should help you with the tiredness and the temperature you've been running."

Drystan and Alistair thanked the healer, then sent him on his way. They both downed the contents of their bottles in one go, and Alistair sighed in relief as the potion did its work. A cooling sensation swept through Drystan, energizing him and cooling his temperature enough to make it bearable.

"Do you really think you could be reaching your full maturity?" Alistair asked, pushing himself up into a sitting position.

Drystan frowned. "I suppose it's possible, but if it's happening to me, why isn't it happening to you?"

Alistair shrugged. "You had sex with her first," he said. "Whereas I did it just yesterday. Judging by your reaction, it seems as though it takes a few days to set in."

Drystan dragged a hand through his hair. "I thought the whole thing about the Dragon's Gift making her mate stronger only applied when they were wed," he said. "I didn't realize it happened through...through..."

"Fucking," Alistair supplied helpfully. "And Lucyan's

having his turn with her right now. I suppose we'll find out in a few days if she has the same effect on all of us."

"And just what does that mean?" Drystan demanded as he got to his feet. "That the Dragon's Gift can strengthen any dragon she beds? That it truly doesn't matter which of us mates with her?"

"I'm not entirely certain why you're getting so bent out of shape about this," Alistair said cautiously as he rose. "It isn't Dareena's fault that this is the way the magic works. Nor is it her fault that our mother birthed three of us rather than one." A sad look crossed his face. "I suspect this is just as hard on her as it is on us."

Drystan blew out a frustrated breath. "It's just...I don't want to have to let her go," he said helplessly. "Even if she picked you instead of me, I'm not sure I could just walk away."

"Same here, brother. Same here."

TWENTY-FOUR

"Do you think this dress is all right, Rona?" Dareena asked nervously as she looked at herself in the mirror. She'd chosen a deep red gown with off-the-shoulder sleeves and a v-neckline. It only showed a bit of cleavage, but it was enough to get the point across and matched the dab of red lip stain on her mouth. There would be no room in Lucyan's mind as to what she intended. And yet...

"I'm worried I'll look like I'm trying too hard."

Rona laughed. "There is no such thing when it comes to Prince Lucyan," she said, her eyes twinkling. "I've seen the women he parades into the Keep—each one more decked out than the last. If anything," she added, plucking at a stray thread hanging from Dareena's sleeve, "you're a bit understated in comparison."

"Understated?" Dareena glanced in the mirror again. Perhaps she was being too modest—there were other, more daring dresses she could wear... "Should I change, then?"

"I wouldn't worry about it," Rona said. "Sometimes less is more, and Prince Lucyan is the one who is trying to woo you, not the other way around. You look just fine."

Dareena sighed deeply, releasing some of the tension in her body. "Thank you, Rona. You may leave now."

Rona bowed, then took herself off to do whatever she did in the Keep when she wasn't tending to Dareena's needs. Alone, Dareena sat down at the small breakfast table where she took her meals and practiced with the flash cards Lucyan had made for her. She hadn't had very much time to drill with them, especially after the brothers had so thoroughly exhausted her the last two days, but she tried to sneak in at least an hour every day, and she was beginning to improve.

"Come in," she called when a knock came at the door. She reorganized the flash cards as Lucyan stepped into the room, looking as handsome as ever in a surcoat of deep blue and gold. His reddish-gold eyebrows rose as she stood up, and she felt another prickle of nerves as he looked her up and down. His amber eyes lingered on her chest for a long moment, and his full lips curved into a smirk that wasn't altogether pleasant.

"So," he drawled, kicking the door closed behind him. "Is it my turn, then?"

Dareena frowned. "Your turn? For what?"

"To bed you." He moved closer, and Dareena swallowed at the dangerous glitter in his eyes. "You slept with Alistair yesterday, Drystan the day before, after I left you. Now that it is my day again, I assume I'm next in line?"

Dareena crossed her arms over her chest, suddenly feeling defensive. "I thought that there were no rules as to how far we could go with each other," she said. "Why are you angry with me?"

Lucyan laughed bitterly, perching on the edge of Dareena's bed much in the same way she had when he'd first come to visit her. "It's strange," he said, shaking his head. "I never thought much about it, but now I understand how all those women felt when they said that they were just another notch in my bedpost. Just a few days ago, you were feeling guilty about letting me touch you—and now suddenly you want to sleep with all three of us?"

Yes—that was definitely anger in his voice. "Lucyan," Dareena said gently, coming over to him. "You are not, and never will be, a notch in my bedpost. I am not trying to 'collect all three princes,' or anything like that. It's just that I don't know how I'm supposed to choose between the three of you if I'm so distracted by sex that I can't truly judge or appreciate your personalities."

"But that's the thing about sex, Dareena," Lucyan said as he took both of her hands in his. "Once you've had it, you always want more. Just look at you. Your entire life, you've been a virgin. Now, in a matter of days, you've had back-to-back sex with Drystan and then Alistair. And now you want me." He yanked her into his lap, leaned in to sniff at her neck. "I can already tell you're getting wet," he murmured into her ear as he burrowed his hand under her skirts to squeeze her bare ass. "Do you really think that, after bedding me, you'll achieve some kind of clarity? Or will you just want to fuck and fuck and fuck?"

Dareena gasped as he slid a finger into her pussy. "Lucyan," she moaned, gripping his shoulders for balance.

"That's right," Lucyan breathed as he slid his finger out, then back in, adding another. "I think you're a dirty girl, Dareena, and that you didn't realize it until you fucked Drystan. I think, deep down inside, you know you'll never get enough. You want me to fill you up, don't you? To ram my cock inside you until it's all you can think about, until you're screaming my name as I fill you with my seed?"

"Yes," Dareena moaned. There was something about the way Lucyan spoke, the way he pumped his fingers into her pussy, that was downright savage. She gasped when he grabbed a fistful of her hair and yanked her head back, then sank his teeth into the sensitive spot where her neck and shoulder met. A bolt of pleasure-pain shot through her, and her pussy clenched so hard around his fingers that he hissed.

"I've never fucked such a tight pussy before," he growled. "Do you think you can take me?"

"I think you're talking too much," Dareena gasped, grabbing the front of his surcoat. She ripped it open, sending brass buttons scattering across the floor. "Are you going to fuck me or not?"

Lucyan threw back his head and laughed. "There's my little spitfire," he said approvingly. He gripped Dareena's waist, then spun around and set her on the bed. "On your hands and knees," he ordered. "Face the door."

Dareena did as he said, her heart hammering with fear and excitement. "Don't you think we should lock the door?" she asked breathlessly as Lucyan flipped her skirt up from behind. "If someone were to walk in..."

"Let them see," he said, and slid his fingers back inside her.

Dareena moaned, arching her back. "What would you do if Drystan or Alistair walked through the door?" His bare chest brushed against her back as he leaned over to whisper in her ear. "Would you scream and bring the blanket up to your chest? Or would you invite them over here to join us?"

"I..." Dareena's mouth went dry at the thought of having *two* brothers in her bed. Her pussy throbbed as she imagined Alistair standing before her, gloriously naked, watching her and Lucyan as he stroked himself. Gods, was she going mad?

"I've never shared a woman with my brothers before," Lucyan said, nipping at her ear. "We dragons are insanely possessive, even of our flings. And yet somehow, I think I would do it for you, if you asked."

He curled his fingers inward, and Dareena cried out as he hit a sweet spot she hadn't realized was inside her. "Yes," she moaned, rocking her hips back to try and increase the friction.

"Uh-uh-uh." Lucyan pulled his fingers out. "I control the pace, not you." He waited until she'd stopped squirming, then slid his fingers back in. "Good girl," he crooned as she moaned again.

Lucyan spent the next twenty minutes torturing Dareena with his skilled fingers. Or at least she thought it was twenty minutes—after a while she lost track, her mind too muddled with lust to make sense of time. Over and over, he brought her to the brink of orgasm, and then pulled back, nibbling at her neck instead, or tracing the shell of her ear with his tongue. Her body shook with need—she was desire personified, eyes wild, skin flushed, hair a tangled mess. All she could think about was

Lucyan's fingers in her pussy, bringing her so close to orgasm and then taking it away again.

"Lucyan," she finally cried, nearly delirious. "Please!"

"Please what?" He pulled his fingers out, then slid them through her folds to find her second sweet spot. "Shall I switch it up? Do you want me to play with your clit instead?" He pinched the sensitive bud, and Dareena screamed in frustration at the pleasure-pain that zinged through her.

"I want...I want..." she panted, trying hard not to strain against his hand as he played with her pussy. She knew that the moment she did, he would pull away—it had already happened three times.

"What do you want?" His mouth was by her ear again. "My tongue?" He licked at her earlobe. "My fingers?" He stroked her clit, his touch featherlight against her swollen flesh. "Or..." She felt something long and hard nudge itself between her ass cheeks. "My cock?"

"Your cock," Dareena moaned. It took everything in her to hold still as he rubbed his shaft along her wet folds. "Lucyan, *please.*"

He pulled away, and for a moment, Dareena was so furious she thought she might actually attack him. But then he surged into her, burying himself to the hilt, and stars exploded behind Dareena's eyes as she was catapulted into an orgasm. She screamed his name as she came, barely noticing when he grabbed a fistful of her hair and pounded into her from behind.

"Fuck," he panted as the sound of flesh slapping against flesh reverberated through the room. "You're incredible." He leaned forward and bit her shoulder, sending another shock of pleasure-pain through her. "I don't care who else you want to fuck," he growled in her ear as he continued to thrust into her, "when we're in bed together, you're *mine.*"

"Yes," she agreed, fisting her hands in the coverlet to keep her balance as the bed shook beneath them. Right now, in this moment, there were no other men. There was only Lucyan, and she was giving herself to him. "Yours."

He groaned loudly into her ear as he spilled himself into her, and Dareena came one more time.

"Lucyan," she said much later as they lounged in the bed together, snacking on a platter of cheese and grapes. They'd made love three more times before Dareena had finally begged off, hungry and exhausted. "Do you think there's something wrong with me?"

Lucyan raised an eyebrow. "If I did, do you think I'd have spent the last three hours buried deep inside you?"

Dareena rolled her eyes and threw a grape at him. "I don't mean physically," she said as he grinned at her. "I mean... shouldn't I feel guilty about sleeping with all three of you? I know my reasons for doing it, and yet...if any woman from the realm saw me now, she would call me a whore. She would say I was cheating." She swallowed against a sudden lump of dread in her throat.

"But you're not cheating." Lucyan wrapped his hand around hers. "You're not cheating, because all four of us agreed to this, together. I know I let my jealousy get the better of me earlier...but that was less about me being upset with you sleeping with my brothers and more about me being annoyed that Drystan got to do it first."

Dareena laughed. "Well, you did give me my first orgasm," she said, plucking another grape and popping it into her mouth. "So you can be proud of that."

"Did I really?" Lucyan's eyes lit up with another one of his grins. "Why didn't you say so in the first place? This entire encounter would have started off much differently."

Dareena snickered. "You're incorrigible."

"Really, though," Lucyan said, sobering up, "despite my initial reaction, you needn't feel guilty about sleeping with any of us. We all agreed that we would do whatever it took to win you, and if that means seeing to your needs, the three of us are happy to oblige."

"Does that mean you really would bring one of your brothers in here if I asked?" Dareena teased.

Lucyan cocked his head. "Is that what you really want?"

Dareena hesitated. "No," she finally said. "I don't see the point." She couldn't deny that the notion intrigued her, but if she could only choose one of them, it seemed cruel to invite more than one into her bed at a time. They would never be allowed to keep up that arrangement once she was officially mated.

She reached for Lucyan again, and he swept what remained of the cheese platter aside, then rolled on top of her for another bout. There was no point in wishing for what could never be, she decided as he slid inside her once again. She might as well spend that time enjoying what she had.

TWENTY-FIVE

Lucyan and Dareena were happily dozing, snuggled together in her tangled bedsheets, when somebody pounded on the door.

"Oh, for gods' sake!" Lucyan grumbled loudly, burying his head beneath a pillow. Dareena moaned, pressing her face against his back. "We're a bit busy here!"

"Well get *un*-busy," Drystan called through the door. "This is important!"

"Drystan?" Dareena called sleepily, lifting her head. She looked like sin incarnate, with her long hair mussed, her green eyes lidded, and her lush lips still swollen from his kisses. "What's going on?"

"Hang on a bloody second," Lucyan snapped, slipping from the bed. He yanked on his trousers and stormed to the door, then opened it a crack. "You two had your day with Dareena already," he snarled. "Why are you interrupting mine?"

"Because we need to speak to you both," Drystan said impatiently, shouldering his way inside. Alistair followed in behind, though at least he had the grace to look apologetic. "Together," Drystan added.

"Together?" Dareena echoed, her gaze flitting between the three brothers. Lucyan sucked in a breath as he realized she was wearing nothing—the sheet had slipped to her waist, exposing her gorgeous breasts.

"Er." Drystan cleared his throat. "You may want to toss on a robe, my lady."

Dareena blushed. "Does my nakedness bother you? I didn't think it mattered since you all have seen me like this now."

"If any one of us were alone with you, it wouldn't," Alistair said, his gentle tone belying the hunger blazing in his eyes. "But seeing you like this...it's going to make it very difficult for us to focus on the conversation at hand."

"Very well." Dareena pulled the sheet up to her chin, then propped some pillows up against her headboard so she could recline against them. "What is it that is so important you two decided to break the rules?" She arched an eyebrow at them.

Lucyan grinned at the sheepish expressions on his brothers' faces. His little minx acted as if she were royalty and they were her subjects, rather than the other way around. He had no doubt she would have all three of them wrapped around her finger, if it hadn't already happened. All three of them would likely do anything to make her happy.

"Alistair and I were sparring earlier today," Drystan said as he took a seat in one of Dareena's chairs. "Both of us ended up needing to be seen by the healer."

"Both of you?" Lucyan rose an eyebrow. "Did you really

come here to tell us that the two of you beat the shit out of each other like you do every week?"

"That's the thing, though," Alistair said, looking troubled. "At first, I was winning the fight. Drystan could barely hit back, and he looked like he was about to faint. Then suddenly his eyes glowed, and he sent me sailing across the room with a single punch."

"A single punch?" Dareena gasped. "Do you two normally hit each other that hard?"

"No," Drystan said grimly. "The three of us are strong, but we have never been capable of such strength before. I cracked two of Alistair's ribs, and so we called the healer to check both of us out. I was feeling very strange, tired and hot, like an old woman with hot flashes or something."

"Of all the ways you've described yourself, that is certainly a new one," Lucyan said dryly. "So, what did the healer tell you? That you shouldn't drink wine before a fight?"

"No," Drystan snapped. "He told me that dragons suffer similar symptoms right before their first shift."

The room went dead silent. "Your first shift?" Lucyan demanded. "What are you talking about? None of us are old enough to shift, not until we..."

He trailed off, looking at Dareena.

"What?" Dareena asked, looking worried. "Is it something I've done?"

"No, darling." Lucyan perched next to her on the bed and stroked her hair. "Nothing on purpose. But traditionally, the only way for a male dragon to shift before his fiftieth birthday is if he mates. It is the gods' way of ensuring that we reproduce in a timely manner, I suspect."

"If...what?" Dareena's mouth dropped open, and her gaze snapped to Drystan. "Does that mean the two of us are mates?"

"I...I would like to believe that," Drystan said, scratching his head. "But the truth is that I don't know. Now that you've bedded all three of us, the same thing could happen to Lucyan and Alistair as well."

"But that doesn't make any sense." Dareena bit her lip. "All three of you can't be my mates. Surely the gods would only make it work for one of you, wouldn't they?"

"I'm not sure," Alistair said uneasily. "I'm feeling a bit strange myself. Nothing like Drystan, but my body temperature has risen some."

Lucyan stared. "And when were you going to mention this?"

"I just did." Alistair folded his arms. "That's why Drystan and I insisted on talking to the two of you now."

"One thing is clear," Drystan said before the two could launch into an argument. "There is more to Shalia's Curse than we know. First, three of us were born when there has only ever been one dragon son in the last nine hundred years. Next, Dareena comes along, and somehow, all three of us have managed to stand here in this room with her while she's naked without tearing each other's throats out."

"I had thought about tearing your throat out when you knocked on the door," Lucyan pointed out.

"Yes, but I'd wager that was more about us interrupting your cuddle time, was it not?" Drystan asked pointedly.

"Face it, Lucyan," Alistair pointed out. "There is something very odd about all of this."

"You said there is more to Shalia's Curse than you know," Dareena said, drawing their attention back to her. "Might we find out more if we take a trip down to the library? Perhaps there are some old scrolls or texts that could illuminate things for us."

Lucyan nodded. "That is an excellent idea," he said. "We'll start tomorrow."

"Tomorrow?" Drystan planted his hands on his hips. "Why not now?"

"You two are certainly welcome to get a head start," Lucyan said, opening the door. "But it is still my day with Dareena, and unless the lady wishes to go down to the library, I plan on staying right here with her."

The three brothers turned toward Dareena as one. "Well?" Drystan demanded. "Are you coming?"

Dareena bit her lip as she looked between them. "I do love visiting the library," she finally said, her gaze resting on Lucyan. "But I made love to your brothers multiple times during their days. To truly test this theory Drystan brought up, it seems that we need to go at least a few more rounds." She arched her back, and the sheet slid down her body again, baring her torso.

All three brothers sucked in a sharp breath.

"You heard the lady," Lucyan said, grabbing Drystan by the elbow. "Away with you." He shoved his protesting brothers out the door, then locked it behind him. True, he might not be jealous that they were eyeing Dareena as if she were their favorite candy, but that didn't mean he wanted an audience while he fucked her.

"Now," he said, turning back to face Dareena. She reclined against the pillows, a broad smile on her face as he joined her back on the bed. "Where would you like to begin?"

TWENTY-SIX

Dareena and the princes spent the next week down in the archives, poring through manuscripts and scrolls for anything that might hint of a way to break the dragon curse. They couldn't stay down there the whole time—the princes had their own duties to attend to, and it would have looked suspicious if they were always down in the library—but they came whenever they could do so safely, and with the princes to help her, Dareena rapidly improved her ability to read dragon runes.

It turned out that Lucyan was right about Dareena's sexual appetites. Though they tried their best not to spend all their time having sex, Dareena found herself on her back with her skirts rolled up at least once a day—sometimes in the library itself, other times in bed, and once even in the stables after she and Alistair had come back from riding. Now that everything was out in the open between them, making love with the brothers was as natural to Dareena as breathing. And the brothers didn't seem to mind sharing, though she'd yet to bed more than one at a time.

"I found something interesting here," she told the brothers as they sat in the library together. "Something that concerns the three of you."

"Oh?" Lucyan lifted an eyebrow. "And what might that be?"

"There's a passage here," she said, tapping the page of the book she had open, "that talks of King Lyrion, one of the early dragon kings. He was only thirty years old when he took the throne, but he was already a full-fledged dragon?"

"He could shift?" Alistair asked, astonished. The brothers all leaned over her shoulder to peer at the manuscript. "But how?"

"It turns out that mating with his Dragon's Gift unlocked his ability to change into dragon form," Dareena said with a sly smile. "It didn't happen instantly, as he was mated to her for a few years before his father passed, but he *was* able to shift."

"I wonder if it has anything to do with how often we make love," Lucyan said, giving her his familiar eyebrow waggle. "Perhaps we should be tossing up your skirts more regularly, my little minx?"

The other brothers rolled their eyes as Dareena giggled. But none of them growled when she leaned in and took Lucyan's mouth in a steamy kiss. "Perhaps we shall," she suggested, trailing a finger down his chest. His nostrils flared, and she knew that he would take her right here in the library if she asked. "After we're done with our research for the day."

The brothers grumbled but acquiesced, returning to their

scrolls. They spent the rest of the afternoon searching, but other than that one tidbit, didn't find anything fruitful.

Later that night, Dareena slipped from her bed, unable to sleep. She left Drystan sleeping soundly and returned to the library to have another look at the archives. Something in her blood told her that she had stumbled upon the right trail—she had already discovered that important bit about King Lyrion. What else might she find?

"Huh." She frowned as she perused yet another tome nearly two hours later. It was a collection of prophecies concerning the dragon kings, handed down through the ages, that she'd found in a remote corner of the library. Some of them talked about things that had already come to pass, while others were nonsensical gibberish that had likely been spouted by a pretended soothsayer rather than a real one. But toward the end, Dareena found one that was oddly specific:

Three together, four as one,
The dragons' curse may be undone.
Three fathers' babe will hold the key
To renewed fertility.

Dareena frowned. Renewed fertility? The dragons' curse? Her heart began to race as she considered the words. Could this be the secret to undoing Shalia's Curse? It certainly seemed to be a direct reference to that. But what was this about three fathers' babe? How could three men father one baby?

Perhaps it's metaphorical, a voice whispered in her head. *There must be some deeper meaning.*

Dareena puzzled over the prophecy for a few more minutes, then gave up with a shake of her head. Grabbing a piece of parchment and a quill, she scribbled it down, then tucked it into the pocket of her robe and gathered up the reading materials she'd taken out. There was no point in going any further—her brain was growing fuzzy with tiredness. Better she come back to it in the morrow, when she was fresh. If she wasn't careful, she might accidentally knock her candle over and burn down the whole library.

Yawning, she returned the last of the scrolls to the shelves, then picked up her candle and prepared to head back to her room. But as she took a step forward a scroll fell to the ground from the top of one of the shelves that was far too high for her to reach. It landed directly in front of her feet, and she forced herself to a halt before she accidentally crushed it with her slipper.

Curious, Dareena bent to pick it up. As she held it up to the candle, which she'd placed back on the shelf, it became obvious that this scroll was different from the others—the parchment was a mottled red, rather than the usual yellowish-white. A tingle ran down her arm as she touched it, and she opened it to see strange, glowing runes inside that she couldn't read.

"Dareena?"

Dareena clapped a hand over her mouth to stifle the involuntary shriek that tore from her throat. Spinning around, she found Drystan standing at the other end of the row.

"By the gods," she gasped, placing a hand against her pounding heart. "You scared the living daylights out of me."

"Sorry." He gave her an apologetic smile. "I woke up to find you missing, so I tracked you here. You couldn't sleep?"

Dareena shook her head. "I came down here to see if I could find anything else about the curse."

"What's that you've got in your hand?" Drystan pointed at the scroll she was holding. "That's some odd-looking parchment."

Dareena held it out to him. "I'm not certain," she said as he took it. "I...I think it might be magic."

"You're bloody right it is," Drystan growled as he studied it. "This is a warlock spell."

"A warlock spell?" Dareena stared. "What is something like that doing down in the archives."

"I don't know. But we're damn well going to find out."

"Well?" Drystan demanded. "What does it say?"

"Hold your damn horses," Lucyan groused as he held the scroll a bit closer to the candlelight. Drystan and Dareena had woken up Alistair, and the three of them had gone to Lucyan's room to see if they could get him to identify the scroll. "It's two in the bloody morning and you've woken me from a dead sleep. My brain needs a little time to catch up."

Drystan grumbled a little, sitting back in his chair. Dareena came around behind Lucyan and rubbed his shoulders as he squinted at the scroll. "Mmm," he said, rolling his neck a bit. "See, that's the kind of attitude we need around here. More helpfulness, less whining."

Alistair raised his eyebrows. "You want us to give you back rubs, Lucyan?"

"Will you stop twisting your neck around and read the scroll?" Drystan demanded. "I want to know what it says."

Lucyan let out a long-suffering sigh, then returned his attention to the scroll. His shoulders tensed as he read it, muttering quietly under his breath. "This...this isn't good."

"What does it say?" Dareena asked.

"It's an assassination spell," Lucyan said. "Meant to make the person look like they fell prey to a mysterious illness."

Alistair stared. "That sounds a lot like..."

"The way Mother died." Drystan gripped the arms of his chair so hard Dareena feared he might break them.

"This doesn't make sense." Lucyan scrubbed a hand over his tired face. "How in the world did a warlock manage to get into the Keep to cast this spell on Mother? And why did he leave this scroll behind, in the archives of all places?"

"You do realize that this points to the warlocks, right?" Alistair said. "Elves wouldn't have done this."

"The elves could have hired a warlock," Drystan pointed out. He shoved up from his chair and began pacing. "We have to tell Father about this."

"I'm not sure that's wise," Lucyan said. "Especially given his propensity for war right now."

"Then what do you suggest we do?" Drystan demanded. "Sweep this under the rug and pretend it didn't happen? *Someone* killed our mother, Lucyan. That someone has to pay."

"Why not call a full council meeting?" Alistair suggested. Everyone turned to look at him—Alistair wasn't usually the idea man. "Drystan is right, we can't just turn the other way. But there's no need to leave this decision solely in Father's hands."

"That may be the smartest thing you've ever said," Lucyan said thoughtfully. "Very well—I'll arrange for it first thing in the morning. Lord Renflaw will be more than happy to grant the request in light of what's happened with the spymaster. But be prepared," he warned. "If Father and the council cannot agree on how to proceed, things could get very ugly."

TWENTY-SEVEN

"This is absolutely *absurd*!"

A ripple of unease went through the council as the king bellowed in Drystan's face. Drystan held his ground, but he couldn't blame the council for being nervous —after all, at the last meeting, one of them had been thrown into the dungeons. Renflaw alone knew the truth about what had happened to Shadley that night; telling him was the only way Lucyan had been able to convince him that they were on his side rather than their father's. Tariana would be returning sometime today, and they would be able to confirm if Shadley had made it to safety.

Even so, a good half of the council seats were empty. Many had begged off or made excuses when Lord Renflaw had sent out the summons. Drystan had hoped that after today's meeting, his father would begin to see sense, but judging by his reaction, that was not likely to happen.

"I can assure you, this scroll is legitimate," Lucyan said. "I visited Shadowhaven once, long before the war started, and visited a spellmaker's shop."

The king scoffed. "Just like you to dabble in black magic," he said, looking down at the scroll in his hand with disgust. "How did the three of you find this, anyway?"

"It was Dareena who found it, actually," Drystan said. "She was looking in the library for something to read and it fell from one of the shelves."

"Of course," the king said, rolling his eyes. "I should have known better than to think my sons would find anything this valuable. A woman had to find it instead."

Drystan ground his teeth together to keep himself from unleashing a scathing retort. "Not just any woman," he said. "She is the Dragon's Gift. I saw what happened when she found it—the scroll fell from one of the top shelves even though nobody had done anything to disturb it. It was almost as if the dragon god himself sent a sign."

"So, you are an augur now, are you?" the king sneered. "Reading signs? Perhaps I should have you shipped off to Targon Temple to train as a priest. Might be the most useful thing I've ever done."

"I am only telling you what I saw," Drystan said stiffly. Targon Temple was located a few miles north of Dragon's Keep on a high mountaintop and was the home of the dragon oracle and his attendants. Priests came to the temple to learn how to serve the dragon god before going back to serve the temples in their own hometowns. Drystan had no intention of trading his formal tunics in for robes or shaving off his crown of hair. He was meant to serve the dragon god as the king, not a priest.

"Regardless of how it happened," Lord Renflaw cut in before the king could taunt him some more, "no one can deny that the scroll exists, and if Lucyan's translation is correct, this may very well have been the weapon used to strike down your mate, my king. If we can get another warlock to corroborate this translation—"

"Don't be a fool," the king snapped. "Doing so would only tip off the warlocks that we are onto them. If they are the enemy, they must not know that we have found out the truth!"

"So you believe me then, Father?" Lucyan asked, sounding a little surprised.

"I know all about your little trip to Shadowhaven," the king said irritably. "You told me you were going on a hunting trip, but I had you followed. Since you didn't do or say anything stupid, I let it slide. It is a good idea for a future king to familiarize himself with the neighboring kingdoms."

Drystan felt a flash of jealousy as he exchanged glances with his brothers. They were all thinking the same thing—had the king made up his mind? Was he going to name Lucyan his successor? He'd said that Dareena would be the one to choose, but everyone knew how capricious their father was. He could change that at any time.

A murmur rippled through the rest of the councilmen. "Does this mean that we'll be going to war against Shadowhaven instead?" one of them said. "And that we can withdraw our troops from elven territory?"

This inspired a rash of other questions, and soon everyone was lobbying strategies and opinions across the table. Some wanted to stop the war entirely, others wanted to turn their forces against the warlocks. Drystan and his brothers said nothing, carefully watching their father for his reaction.

Finally, the king slammed his fist on the table. "Enough!" he roared, silencing everyone else. "Have the rest of you gone mad?"

"Gone mad?" Lord Renflaw sputtered, and Drystan knew he was barely keeping himself from spouting off about the irony of the king calling *him* mad. "Why would you say such a thing, my king?"

"It is clear," the king said in a voice like ice, "that you have all forgotten your history. Yes, Shadowhaven may have been responsible for my mate's death. But who were they allied with in the last war?"

"Elvenhame," one of the councilmen said after a protracted silence.

"Exactly," the king spat. "Those filthy elves are no less our enemy now than they have always been. We will not be withdrawing our troops from Elvenhame's borders, not until we've conquered them. Then, and *only* then, will we march on Shadowhaven."

He stormed from the room, leaving the councilmen to stare after him, speechless. Drystan and his brothers exchanged helpless glances—this was worse than they could have imagined. They'd hoped to stop the bloodshed—instead, they'd given the king a reason to go after *two* kingdoms, not just one.

"Your father," Renflaw said faintly, once the king was out of earshot, "is insane."

"You don't have to tell us that," Alistair muttered.

They stayed with the council for a while longer, trying to

come up with a way to get the king to listen. But several hours of back and forth had produced nothing—the councilmen were too afraid for their lives to directly oppose the king, and Drystan and his brothers could not see a way to penetrate their father's madness long enough for him to see reason. They left the room together, utterly defeated, and were halfway down the hall when someone came running up behind them.

"Tariana!" Drystan exclaimed as his sister grabbed him by the arm and pulled him to a stop. "Did you just arrive?"

"Back in time to miss the council meeting, I see," Lucyan said dryly. "Although perhaps it's best you did, considering how it went."

"What's wrong?" Alistair asked, noting, as Drystan did, the grim set of Tariana's features. "Did something go awry after you left?" Tension filled the air, and Drystan's stomach tightened with nerves. Had Shadley been killed, or worse, captured?

"Everything went according to plan," Tariana said in a voice that suggested otherwise. "But we really need to talk."

TWENTY-EIGHT

While the brothers were shut up in the council meeting, Dareena decided to pay a visit to Targon Temple. Donning her best dress, she set off in a carriage with a guard, clutching the small piece of paper she'd written the prophecy on. The carriage bumped and jostled around the dirt road that wound up the mountainside, and she stared out at the passing trees and wildlife, her chest wound tight with nerves.

She'd wanted to discuss it with the brothers before they went to the council meeting, but she hadn't wanted to burden their minds with yet another puzzle. Nor did she want them to get their hopes up in case her suspicions were wrong. No, it was better to go to the temple first to pray to the dragon god for guidance. With any luck, her status as the Dragon's Gift would allow her to speak with the oracle, and he would give her the guidance she needed to move forward.

"We're here, my lady," the guard said as the carriage rolled to a stop.

Dareena nodded. She surreptitiously tucked the note into her skirt pocket, then allowed the guard to help her out of the carriage. Smoothing her skirts, she took a deep breath as she looked around.

Targon Temple was the most sacred place in all of Dragonfell, and Dareena could feel it even standing outside. Usually forests were alive with sound, but in this small clearing, there was a hushed reverence, the only sounds the snapping of twigs beneath their shoes and the gentle trickle of a stone fountain carved in the shape of a dragon. A few parishioners were standing around it, washing their hands and mouths before entering the temple, as was customary.

Wrapping her shawl tighter around her, Dareena turned toward the temple. It was a massive structure, two stories tall and constructed of wooden beams painted a brilliant vermillion —the color of dragon's fire—with golden runes shimmering along some of them. The building material seemed an odd choice, since wood was so flammable, but then again, they were in the middle of a forest. Marble or granite would have been very difficult to bring up the mountainside.

"My lady?" the guard asked. "Are you ready to go inside?"

Dareena nodded. She approached the fountain with the guard and used one of the wooden ladles to scoop up the water. She sucked in a breath as the chilly water splashed over her hands. This high up the mountain, the temperature was far colder. Hurriedly, she cleaned her hands, then swished the water in her mouth and spit it into the gutter that ran along the bottom edge of the fountain. The guard handed her a fresh handkerchief when she was finished, and she used it to dry her hands, then stuck them beneath her armpits to warm them.

Finished, she climbed the steps to the temple, then toed off her shoes and handed them to a waiting attendant. Barefoot, she stepped onto one of the woven rugs that covered the entire wooden floor, thankful for the bit of insulation. Each rug was embroidered with a border of dragons, and Dareena was careful to always step in the middle of the rug lest she offend the god.

On the other side of the main temple floor was a shrine with a statue of the dragon god and various offerings gathered around him. Dareena took the bottle of fire wine she'd brought from the guard and handed it to another attendant before kneeling in front of the dragon's effigy.

Closing her eyes, she clasped her hands together and prayed for guidance. In the silence of her mind, she told the dragon god all about Drystan, Lucyan, and Alistair, the three men that the king had mandated her to choose between as her husband, and the one to continue the dragon line. She talked about each of their personalities—how Drystan was stern, but tender, and spent more sleepless nights worrying about the fate of the kingdom than anyone else knew. How Lucyan, beneath all his smirks and games, secretly had a heart of gold, and sincerely hoped no one would ever find out. And how Alistair never abandoned his principles or pretended to be anything other than what he was.

How am I supposed to choose? she asked the dragon god. *How can I decide to love one more than the others?*

Because she did love them all. Fiercely. And she couldn't

stand to break any of their hearts by rejecting one in favor of the other.

Dareena had hoped that because of her status as the Dragon's Gift, the dragon god might speak to her. But though she briefly felt a presence brush against the edges of her mind, she heard no divine voice. There would be no easy answers, then. She would have to tread this path alone.

Sighing, she opened her eyes. As the guard helped her to her feet, she felt a familiar tingle, the one she always felt when someone was watching her. Turning, she saw the oracle standing to the side. He looked exactly the same as he had last time, his hands tucked into his voluminous vermillion and white robes, his face the picture of serenity.

"Good morning, my lady," he said in a hushed voice as she approached. "You wanted to visit with me?"

"I did," Dareena said with a smile. She wondered if he'd divined their meeting, or if he'd simply made an educated guess. It was likely the latter, but still, there was an air of mystery about the oracle that could not be denied. "I am in need of guidance. I was hoping we might talk in private?"

The oracle nodded, then led her to a private garden in the back. They sat on a stone bench in front of a small pond surrounded by fragrant perennials. A butterfly fluttered past, and Dareena reached out. It perched on her finger for a moment, allowing her to admire its shimmering wings, then floated off to sip from the garden's bountiful nectar. Her guard stood at a discreet distance near a group of tall liatris, close enough to spring into action should anything happen but far enough to be out of earshot.

"Well, we are alone now," the oracle said. "What is it you wish to speak to me about?"

Dareena hesitated, her fingers wrapping around the scrap of paper in her pocket. "I am not certain if you heard of the king's decree regarding which of his sons is to be my husband?"

"I have." The oracle nodded. "He wishes you to choose for yourself. An odd decision, and yet I believe that is the dragon god's will. Divinity runs within your veins, or you would not have become the Dragon's Gift, Dareena Sellis. Our god will guide you when the time comes to make a decision."

"But that's just it," Dareena said helplessly. "I can't make a decision. I care for all three brothers equally. And...and I think that maybe I'm not meant to."

"Not meant to?" For the first time, the oracle's serene expression vanished. His brow furrowed as he stared at Dareena. "Of course you are meant to choose. You are the Dragon's Gift. You cannot reject them all."

"That isn't what I meant." Frustrated, Dareena finally pulled the paper from her skirt pocket. "I found this when I was reading through a book of prophecies about the dragon kings. I think it's about me and the princes."

Frowning, the oracle took the paper from Dareena. His eyes widened as he scanned the words, and all the color drained from his face.

"Oracle?" Dareena asked hesitantly, unsure how to interpret his reaction. "Is everything all right?"

"This...this is heresy!" he hissed, color rushing back into his face and turning it bright red. "This should never have been published!"

"What are you doing!" Dareena cried as he tore the paper in two. She tried to snatch it back from him, but he twisted away and ripped it up into pieces. Her guard rushed forward at the sound of her distress, but she held up a hand to ward him off as the tiny pieces of parchment floated away on the wind. A lump swelled in her throat, but she held back the tears as the oracle panted, both of them fighting for composure.

"Why," she finally said when she trusted her voice enough to speak again, "did you do that?"

"What you just read was nonsense." The oracle had resumed his serene expression, his voice steady as the surface of a frozen lake. "The soothsayer who wrote that prophecy was known for her spells of madness. All of her prophecies were supposed to have been stricken from that book. It seems that we missed one of them."

Dareena stared. "Are you certain?" she asked. "That prophecy is so specific—she seems to be talking directly about us—"

"You dare question me?" Anger flashed in the oracle's eyes again, and for a split second, Dareena feared he might actually strike her. Surely he wouldn't, with her guard so close by? But her hand drifted toward her knife again as a tremor of unease filled her. There was something not quite right about this man—something that lurked beneath his aura of serenity.

But the anger in the oracle's eyes faded away, and he gently patted her shoulder. "I forgive you for your impertinence, my lady," he said in a soft voice. "We often speak out of turn in times of turmoil, and you have experienced your fair share recently. But you must forget about this nonsense. It is imperative that you pick your mate, and soon. The dragon line must continue."

Dareena nodded, slowly rising from the stone bench. "Thank you for your guidance," she said, bowing her head. "I appreciate you taking the time to visit with me."

"Any time," the oracle said, getting to his feet as well. "It is always a pleasure to serve the Dragon's Gift."

Dareena curtsied, then allowed her guard to escort her back to her waiting carriage. Questions whirled in her mind as the carriage began its journey down the mountainside again, more questions than she could ever hope to answer. But one thing was absolutely certain in her mind.

The oracle was lying.

TWENTY-NINE

"All right," Lucyan said as he shut the door to his suite. "Enough of the suspense. Tell us what happened, Tariana."

He turned to where his sister sat, her boots crossed at the ankles, her arms folded across her chest. She looked exhausted, shadows thick beneath her amber eyes, and even though she was not Lucyan's favorite person, he felt a moment's pity for her.

"The war is not going our way," Tariana said as Alistair handed her a drink. He handed one to the rest of them too—a fine aged whiskey that Lucyan had been saving for a special occasion, but what the hell? Talking about all the ways their lives were fucked seemed just as good a reason as any to drink the stuff. "We are about to lose it."

"I thought we were in a stalemate, but pushing forward," Drystan said. "That *is* what you told Father at the last council meeting."

"We *have* been, but that is about to end," Tariana said.

"Elvenhame's army is twice as large as ours—they could have crushed us like an ant a long time ago, and they are preparing to do exactly that."

Alistair scowled. "That doesn't make any sense. Why would Elvenhame have waited so long to destroy us if they've had the capability to do so all along."

"Because," Lucyan said, the answer slapping him in the face. Gods, how could he not have seen this? "You've been fucking that pretty elven prince of yours, haven't you?"

Tariana's face colored. "Watch your mouth, or I'll smack the teeth out of *your* pretty face."

Lucyan batted his eyelashes. "You think I'm pretty?"

"Enough!" Drystan snapped. His eyes sparked with anger as he looked at Tariana. "Is this true, sister? You really have been in bed with the enemy this whole time?"

"Ryolas is *not* the enemy!" Tariana snapped back. "He and I are the only reason that our troops are still alive."

"Of course," Alistair muttered. "The two of you have been rigging the battles. No wonder we've suffered so little loss of life."

"Rigging the battles?" Drystan echoed. "How is that even possible?"

"Let me guess," Lucyan drawled as the picture unfolded in his mind's eye. "You've been restricting the attacks and counter-attacks to relatively remote areas to ensure that they have as limited an effect on the citizens as possible. You've also been exchanging prisoners, which explains why we've had no elven officers to torture recently."

"You always were the clever one, little brother," Tariana said, giving Lucyan a humorless smile. "Yes, Ryolas and I have been working in concert to minimize casualties until the three of you were finally mated and powerful enough to overthrow our father. The elves had nothing to do with it, and Ryolas and I are both loath to see Dragonfell decimated over a misunderstanding."

Drystan shook his head. "I can't believe you didn't tell us about this. When were you going to let us know that you wanted us to depose Father? Were you just going to spring that on us at the last minute?"

"Is this the real reason you've kept me from the front lines?" Alistair demanded. "Because you were afraid I would find out the truth?"

"I couldn't risk any of you knowing," Tariana said. To her credit, she at least looked apologetic, though that didn't quell Lucyan's anger. In truth, he was angrier at himself than his sister—he should have figured this out. Clearly, he had a long way to go in his spymaster career. "Father has all three of you under his thumb. He may be mad, but he is still very good at manipulating others to serve his interests at the expense of their own."

"Not as good as you think," Lucyan growled. He pulled the spell scroll from his sleeve, which he'd snatched after his father had tossed it onto the table and stormed from the meeting room. "Dareena found this in the library."

Tariana's eyes widened as she took it from him. "A spell scroll in the library?" she asked as she unfurled it. "Why in Terragaard would such a thing be in our castle?"

"It appears to be an assassination spell," Lucyan said in a clipped voice. "We believe it was used to kill our mother."

Tariana's face went white. "I knew it," she spat, allowing the scroll to snap shut. "Those bastard warlocks and their black magic. They've always been jealous of our superior resources."

"We called a council meeting today and showed them the scroll," Alistair said. "Father believes us, but he won't call off the attack on Elvenhame. He still believes they are the enemy, and since he is under the false impression that we have enough men to defeat them, he intends to continue the war."

Tariana let out a disgusted sigh. "Well, that is about to come to an end," she said. "I met with Ryolas today. His father is beginning to suspect our ruse. He fears that the High King will replace him with his older brother, who has no qualms about crushing us. The elves as a whole are not sympathetic to our plight, not when it appears that history is repeating itself."

"Fuck." Lucyan raked a hand through his hair. "How much time do you think we have until that happens?"

Tariana shrugged. "It could be a week. It could be tomorrow. All I know is that if we don't figure out a way to get Father to surrender, there won't be a Dragon Force when they're through with us."

"Forget the Dragon Force," Alistair muttered. His eyes, usually so full of optimism, were bleak. "If the elvish forces are as large as you claim, there won't *be* a Dragonfell left by the time they're through with us."

THIRTY

After Dareena returned from her visit with the oracle, she headed back to the library with the intention of doing more research on the curse. But as she stood amongst the stacks, trying to figure out where she wanted to start, she realized her heart wasn't in it. What was the point in searching for answers when even the oracle had stonewalled her?

She hadn't been able to find the brothers, but she'd flagged down Lord Renflaw on his way out of the Keep, and he'd told her what had happened. As usual, the king refused to listen to reason. Even if she *did* find something more substantial than that prophecy, the king would just dismiss anything she found out of hand on account of her being nothing but a broodmare.

Heat rose to Dareena's cheeks, and she clenched her fists. She'd wanted to rake her nails across the king's smug face when he'd said that to her. When she'd first come to Dragon's Keep, she wouldn't have dared contemplate such a thought, but her time with the brothers had taught her that she was not just a simple commoner. The princes found her smart and funny, and their constant praise and adoration had done wonders for her self-confidence.

No, she was not the serving girl who had left Hallowdale all those weeks ago. She was the Dragon's Gift, and she mattered.

Closing the book she'd taken from the shelf, she decided to seek out the brothers again. She could take a break from the stacks for one day. Right now, she just wanted to spend some quality time with someone who cared for her and forget about the king and his nasty words.

She was about to round the corner when someone slapped a hand across her mouth and yanked her around. Her muffled scream froze in her throat as she saw the king—he pinned her up against the wall, his cruel mouth bared in a snarl as he towered over her. Waves of fury rolled off him, turning Dareena's blood to ice and her legs to water. Oh gods. Was he going to kill her?

"Scream, and you'll be spending the next six months in the dungeon, choking down gruel," he rasped in her ear. "Do you understand?"

Dareena nodded, tears stinging her eyes. The king removed his hand from her mouth, but he kept her backed up against the wall, barely an inch of space between their bodies. "What do you want?" she asked, her voice breathless with terror. Her hand inched toward the slit in her skirt, where the jade knife Drystan had bought her was hidden. "I haven't done anything wrong."

"Don't try to play me for a fool, whore," the king spat, his amber eyes blazing with anger. "You aren't the first woman who's tried to pull the wool over my eyes, nor will you be the last. I see right through your innocent act, and if you ever try to pit my sons against me again, I will send my Dragon Force to the hovel you came from and kill every friend or acquaintance you've ever had."

"P-please," Dareena stammered, thinking of poor Gilma. She wouldn't stand a chance if the Dragon Force came for her, and neither would Tildy. They might even come for Mr. Harrin, and while things had gone bad between them in the end, he'd still helped her when no one else would. "There's no need to hurt anyone."

"No," the king crooned, the cruel expression melting into something that turned Dareena's stomach. He reached up and brushed the backs of his knuckles across Dareena's cheek. "There isn't, is there? I think you and I both know there's a better way. We don't have to be enemies, Dareena. Together, you and I could conquer the world."

He leaned in to brush his lips against hers, and Dareena's hand closed around the handle of her knife. She trembled as she prepared to yank it out, certain that what she was about to do would spell her doom, and yet she couldn't just stand here and let the king do this, she couldn't—

"Father?" Alistair's voice echoed down the hall. "What are you doing?"

The king's gaze shuttered, and he pulled back. "Just having a friendly conversation with my future daughter-in-law," he said as Dareena let go of the knife handle. Alistair looked between them curiously, and Dareena forced her features into a blank expression. It took everything she had not to collapse to the floor in relief, but she couldn't let on that anything was amiss. "I'm trying to get her to tell me which one of you she plans to choose...but alas, the wench's lips are sealed."

"That's too bad," Alistair said, looping his arm through Dareena's. "I've been wondering that too. I'm afraid we must be off now—I promised Dareena we'd take a walk in the gardens together. With your leave, of course." He bowed, and Dareena forced herself to follow suit.

"Of course." The king's eyes glittered. "Enjoy your stroll."

Dareena said nothing as Alistair gently steered her up the hall. Her heart was still pounding, her body trembling. The king had come so close, so close—

"Shhh." Alistair pulled her into a deserted parlor room and shut the door behind them. "It's all right," he said as Dareena began to cry, and he gathered her into his arms. "You're safe now."

"I was going to stab him, Alistair," she sobbed into his chest as he held her tight. "He was about to rape me, and I was going to stab him."

"I wouldn't blame you if you did," Alistair said as he gently rocked Dareena in his arms. "My father is a rank bastard. But he is also the king. From now on, you must never leave your room without an escort. Make sure you are always with us, or if not, with your maid."

"My maid isn't always available, and neither are you," Dareena said, sniffling. "You can't protect me all the time."

"The hell I can't," Alistair growled. He wiped Dareena's tears away, then gave her a gentle kiss. "Maybe not by myself, but between me and my brothers there is no reason for you to be alone. You'll sleep in one of our beds from now on so that you're never alone at night, and one of us will be with you at all times during the day. We'll protect you, Dareena. On my life, I swear it."

Dareena swallowed, her fear finally fading. "Thank you, Alistair," she said, cupping his cheek. "You're always so sweet to me."

Alistair smiled. "I'm just trying to serve my lady," he said softly, pulling her close again. He kissed her tenderly, and Dareena sighed, the tension bleeding away. Drystan made her feel powerful, Lucyan drove her wild, but Alistair—he was the one who calmed her soul, who soothed her nerves and banished her fears with his gentle touches and kind smiles. It was an odd contradiction, as he was the soldier of their bunch, but though Alistair was a warrior on the outside, he had the heart of a poet.

Wrapping her arms around his neck, Dareena let Alistair bring her to the couch and soothe the stress and terror of the past few minutes away. Here in Alistair's arms, she was safe. The king wouldn't barge in here and try to take her again.

"I'm glad you've returned," Alistair said once her heartbeat had slowed and her tears were gone. "I know you've just been through an ordeal, but we have much to talk about."

Dareena sighed. "I already heard from Lord Renflaw. The king is not going to cease his attack on Elvenhame. He will defeat them and then go on to attack Shadowhaven."

Alistair laughed bitterly. "Except he isn't. Our king thinks he has the numbers necessary to overtake Elvenhame, but we have been facing only a fraction of their force. The elves may soon crush us if we don't convince Father to surrender or negotiate a truce."

Dareena frowned, pulling back so she could look into Alistair's eyes. The despair she saw in them made her feel sick. "What do you mean, we've only been facing a fraction of their force? How could we have been so grossly misinformed about their army?"

Alistair sighed. "Because Tariana's been playing a deadly game of chess with the enemy."

He explained to her all about how Tariana and Prince Ryolas were working together to minimize casualties, but that the High King of the elves was catching on and there was a real danger Ryolas would be removed from command. Dareena's veins filled with icy horror as the situation became quite clear—if they did not stand down, Dragonfell would be destroyed, and the last of the dragon line along with it.

"That is *it*!" She jumped to her feet, her heart racing as she paced around the room. "We cannot just stand aside and let your father lead our kingdom to ruin."

Alistair raised his eyebrows. "I agree," he said slowly, rising from the couch. "But there is nothing we can do to stop him. Even when you choose one of us, which is inevitable"—a hint of bitterness crept into his tone—"our father will still be king until your mate is strong enough to challenge him, or until he dies."

"And yet," Dareena said, coming to a stop and trailing a hand down Alistair's muscular forearm, "you and Lucyan have been going through the same changes as Drystan, haven't you? I've noticed the mood swings and the irritability."

Alistair nodded. "We have been getting stronger."

Dareena smiled, then rose up on her tiptoes to kiss him. "Call your brothers here. I think I have a plan that can finally end this madness once and for all."

THIRTY-ONE

The last few days of the final week went by in a blur. Every day they trained, every night they made love, and all the while, they clung to the hope that Dareena's plan would work. That she hadn't misinterpreted the prophecy, and that they would convince the king to step down and let them take over.

Dareena knew the brothers wanted to end this peacefully, without bloodshed. She sincerely hoped she could give them that gift. Their father might have gone off the deep end, but he was still family. The bond between father and son was not easily broken, even by such a powerful force as madness. With any luck, King Dragomir would remember that bond, and would do the right thing.

For the most part, they tried not to think about what could go wrong, and focused on making sure that everything went right. But all too soon, the big day came—the day when Dareena would stand before the king and all of his courtiers and finally announce which of the princes she'd chosen as heir to the Drag-onfell throne.

"You look stunning, my lady," Rona gushed as she stepped back. She'd brought a special dress out just for the occasion—a sleek gown of gold and white that hugged her curves in the right places. Gold jewelry dangled at her ears, her Dragon's Gift collar curled around her throat, and her hair was left to hang loose down her back. It was the perfect combination of innocent and sexy.

"You did a wonderful job with this dress, Rona." Dareena skimmed a hand down the silken fabric of the skirt, wondering if it would still be this pristine by the time the day was ended.

"Thank you." Rona beamed. "Are you ready, my lady? I hope you don't feel too nervous."

"Not at all." Dareena smiled even though that was the furthest thing from the truth. Her stomach was a roiling, greasy ball of nerves—she'd barely been able to choke down her break-fast this morning, and now she regretted eating at all. What if she was wrong? What if the plan failed, and everything they'd strived so hard for came crashing down around their ears?

Stop thinking that way, she scolded herself. *You're only making things worse. How are the princes going to have faith in you when you have no faith in yourself?*

Dareena forced herself to calm down, taking slow, even breaths. She fingered the stone on her mother's ring, which she'd worn on her right hand today. The cool white stone comforted her, slowing her heartbeat and drying the sweat that had started gathering in her palms. A guard came to escort her, and she kept a neutral expression on her face as he led her to the audience chamber, where the king and his sons were waiting. Just as last time, he sat in his throne with his sons to his left and his daughters to his right, but unlike last time, the galley seats were filled to the brim with nobles, the hall buzzing with excited conversation. The chatter faded as Dareena slowly approached the dais, and she did her best to ignore all the eyes on her as she curtsied deeply before the throne.

"My king," she said, her voice low and respectful, not a hint of the anger and betrayal that sizzled in her veins.

"Rise," the king said, and she did. The room fell silent, and Dareena could practically feel the air humming with anticipation. This was it. The moment they'd been waiting on tenterhooks for.

"Dareena Sellis of Hallowdale," the king boomed in a loud voice, his eyes glittering. "You are the Dragon's Gift, sent to us by the gods themselves to wed the future dragon king. Who amongst my sons have you chosen to further the dragon line with? Who amongst them is worthy of being my successor?"

Dareena turned to look at the princes. They stood solemnly, their hands clasped behind their backs, and for a second, she hesitated. There was no reason to do this. She could simply choose one of them, and things could go on the way they were originally meant to. They could bide their time, wait until they were stronger.

But Lucyan winked at her, and that tiny show of confidence evaporated the hesitation. The princes were counting on her—no, the kingdom was counting on her. She would not fail them.

Dareena took a deep breath and squared her shoulders. "I choose all of them," she said in a loud voice that carried through the entire hall. "The gods have blessed you with three sons to continue your line, and I will serve them all."

Gasps of shock echoed in the hall, and the nobles began whispering amongst themselves. "This is blasphemy!" the king cried, his cheeks mottling with anger. "The Dragon's Gift has never before served as consort to more than one male. This is unheard of!"

"That is only because there has never been more than one son in line for the throne, my king," Dareena said. "Or at least, it has been that way since your line was cursed."

"Silence!" the king thundered, and the room went utterly still. "I'll pretend you never uttered such a disgusting thing from your whorish mouth. Now tell me who you've chosen, or gods help me, I will make the choice for you."

"She has already made her choice," Drystan said as he and his brothers flanked Dareena. "She has chosen all of us, and in turn, we choose her."

The king laughed. "And what, the three of you are to become her little menagerie now, is that it? She's got you more firmly beneath her thumb than I thought." Sneering, he rose from his throne. "Since the three of you aren't man enough to tame the whore standing before you, I shall take it upon myself to do so. Dareena Sellis shall become my consort, and she will bear me sons far better than the likes of you three!"

More gasps of shock echoed through the hall, the gallery absolutely scandalized by what they were hearing. Dareena wasn't certain which notion appalled them most—the idea of Dareena marrying the king, or marrying all three brothers at once.

"The hell you will!" Lucyan snarled, pulling Dareena behind him. "You've had your filthy paws on her once already, Father. I'll not let you do so again."

"Please." Alistair approached the dais, splaying his hands wide in a gesture of peace. "We don't wish to quarrel with you, Father. We only want what is ours by right."

"And what do you think that is?" the king barked. "The throne?" He threw back his head and laughed. "None of you deserve it."

Before any of the princes could respond, the king drew a dagger from his belt and flung it straight at Alistair. Alistair tried to dodge, but the blade sank into his shoulder, and he roared in pain. The brothers drew their swords and charged, and Dareena threw herself to the ground as the king spewed a gout of fire from his breast.

"Out!" Tariana shouted as the hall erupted into pandemonium. She grabbed Dareena by the arm and hauled her through the exit. Terror banded around Dareena's chest as she looked back to see King Dragomir shifting, his human body morphing into a giant dragon with shimmering green scales. His tail lashed this way and that, flinging furniture about while the guards rushed to evacuate everyone from the hall. One woman was hit in the back of the head by a crystal ornament as she fled, and she went down on the floor in a heap. Two men rushed to grab her and get her out before she got hit again.

"Lucyan!" Dareena cried as the king's tail slammed into his torso. He crashed into the opposite wall, then went down in a heap, tangled up with the banner. Dareena tried to run toward him, but Tariana hauled her through a side door, then slammed it shut.

"There's nothing you can do," she panted. "You'll only be in the way if you stay."

Dareena's eyes burned as she allowed Tariana to lead her away from the battle. She wished there was something more she could do for the brothers, but in the past week, she'd done all she could to strengthen them. It was up to them to use their power to subdue the king.

If they failed, they were all doomed.

THIRTY-TWO

"**D**ammit!" Drystan yelled as Lucyan crumpled to the ground. His brother was pale as death beneath the blood-red tapestry he'd brought down with him, and his eyes were closed. "Lucyan, wake up!"

He raced toward his brother, trying to get to him before his father could crush him. There was no humanity left in King Dragomir's eyes now; he wouldn't hesitate to kill them all. The king turned toward their fallen brother, his talons already coming down—

"Oh no you don't!" Alistair cried. He plunged his sword into their father's left flank. The king's roar of pain and rage shook the walls, and as he whipped around to face their youngest brother, something in Drystan finally snapped. Fire surged through his veins, stronger, hotter than ever, and he screamed in pain and anger as his body seemed to splinter apart from the inside. Everything was twisting...changing...

Shifting, Drystan realized with awe as his field of vision grew broader. His neck and spine lengthened as wings sprouted from his back, and his hands and feet grew talons. Shimmering blue scales covered his newly formed body, and suddenly he could see a multitude of colors that hadn't been visible to his human eyes before.

His father's murderous gaze faltered, anger giving way to surprise. For a moment, Drystan caught a flash of what looked like pride in them. His father was still in there.

And yet, it was too late to go back. Too late to do anything but plow forward.

Roaring, Drystan launched himself at his father. The two crashed straight through the enormous glass window behind the dais and tumbled down the hillside. Drystan howled as his father's claws dug into him, and he did the same, clinging to the bastard for dear life. If he let go, his father would get airborne, and he would be fucked.

But it seemed there was no stopping that. The king sank his talons deep into Drystan's upper arms, then snapped out his wings and lifted off. Drystan struggled to release his father's grip before they got too high, but the landscape shrank rapidly as they gained altitude. Dragon's Keep and the surrounding city grew into tiny pinpricks. Panic surged through Drystan, and he lashed out with his tail, aiming for his father's wings. He managed to slash at one with his spikes, and the king snarled as the thick membrane tore. Encouraged, Drystan did it a second time, this time aiming for the second wing. He missed the wing, but the spike on the end of his tail stabbed his father in the eye instead.

The king's roar of pain seemed to shake the very sky, and his talons finally loosened from Drystan's hide. Drystan's heart leapt into his throat as he plummeted toward the ground. At first, he didn't know what to do, but instinct kicked in, and his wings snapped out. He flapped them, trying to push himself up to where his father was, but they were too weak. He was forced to glide on the winds, leaving his back as a giant target for his father to land on.

Except he didn't. Looking up, Drystan saw that his father wasn't coming for him. Instead, he was flying away, heading straight for the Black Mountains at the western border.

Drystan couldn't believe it. Their father was actually running away.

Clenching his jaw, Drystan did his best to bank toward the hillside where the keep was perched. He could feel hundreds of eyes on him as he closed in, citizens pointing and gawking at the newest dragon in their midst. Even though dragons ruled here, it was still a rare sight to see one. The king usually only shifted for the public a few times a year—the rest of the time, when he wanted to hunt as a dragon, he waited until he was already outside the city limits before he changed forms.

But that was the old King Dragomir. The new one had shifted right in the middle of the throne room, endangering the lives of his subjects as he'd tried to kill his own sons.

And all because he couldn't bear to give up his crown.

"Drystan!" Dareena cried as he landed on the hillside. He lifted his head to see her running down the hillside, the skirts of her dress clutched in one hand. Tariana and Alistair were right on her heels, twin expressions of shock and relief on their faces.

Exhaustion rippled through Drystan, and just like that, he

shifted back into human form. Naked, he collapsed to the ground, his vision hazy. The shifting, the fighting, the flying—all of it had drained his strength away.

"You did it," Alistair said as Dareena dropped to his side. "You actually fucking did it."

Drystan grinned up at his brother as Dareena stroked his back. His wounds had healed during the shift, but there was still some residual pain, and her touch felt soothing. "Someone had to do it," he said.

Alistair rolled his eyes. "I was about to, but you seemed like you had things in hand."

"Hardly," Tariana said, looking toward the horizon. Drystan knew her gaze was fixed on their father's retreating form. "He's going to come back, you know."

"And we'll be ready for him when he does," Dareena said as she slung an arm over Drystan's shoulder. She helped him to his feet, and Alistair offered him a cloak to wrap around his aching body. "The three of you will only get stronger as you continue to train. You'll have to add flying practice to your list of things to accomplish," she said with a smile as she kissed Drystan's cheek. He chuckled at her ability to find humor even in a dire moment like this. "The last thing we need is for you to plant your face in the ground again."

"Indeed." Drystan looked toward the Keep. "Is Lucyan all right?" he asked, his stomach clenching as he remembered how his father had smashed his brother into the wall.

"He's been taken to the infirmary," Tariana said grimly. "I believe he only has a few broken bones—nothing life-threatening. But he'll need a day or two to recover."

"Tariana," Alistair said slowly, getting all of their attention as he pointed toward the sky. "Is that Solara?"

Everybody turned to where Alistair was pointing. "Solara shouldn't be here," Tariana said, her face paling as they watched the dragon approach. "She is supposed to be running the troops in my absence."

Solara's red scales glinted in the morning sun as she flapped her wings, and within moments, she was touching down on the ground. "Bad news," she panted after she'd shifted back into human form. She yanked a cloak out of the pack tied around her wrist and wrapped it around her naked body as she spoke. "Prince Arolas has taken over Elvenhame's army. He's killed and imprisoned half our forces. We're preparing for another battle, but it'll be our last."

"Half our forces?" Alistair echoed, the horror in his voice echoing Drystan's perfectly. Thousands dead or in chains...he felt sick to his stomach as he imagined the battlefield soaked with Dragonfell blood.

"Are any of our sisters among the dead?" Tariana demanded. She grabbed Solara by the shoulder when she did not immediately answer. "How many?"

"Three." Solara's eyes grew bright with unshed tears. "And two are badly wounded."

"*Fuck*." Tariana clenched her fists at her sides, trembling with anger. "You said Arolas is leading Elvenhame's army now. What of Ryolas?"

"I don't know," Solara said, shaking her head. "He's likely been arrested and is rotting in a dungeon. He's certainly in no position to help us, and Arolas is out for blood. He'll slaughter us if we meet him on the field."

"There's no need for a battle," Drystan protested. "We're more than happy to stand down. Our father just abandoned the throne. It is within our power to negotiate a surrender."

"That's all well and good," Solara said wearily, "but the time for negotiating is past. The High King is sending an envoy here. They'll be at our door in a matter of hours. He wants a hostage in exchange for sparing the soldiers he's taken prisoner."

"A hostage?" Tariana asked as a terrible feeling settled in Drystan's chest. "Has he said who?"

"He has." Solara met Dareena's wide emerald eyes, and Drystan tightened his arm around her, holding her close. She couldn't mean what she was about to say. She just couldn't.

"No," Alistair growled, stepping in front of Dareena. "Over my dead body."

"Yes," Solara said grimly. "He wants the Dragon's Gift."

To be continued...

Dareena's story continues in DRAGON'S BLOOD, Book 2 of The Dragon's Gift trilogy. Make sure to join the mailing list so you can be notified of future release dates, and to receive special updates, freebies and giveaways!

CLICK HERE TO JOIN

Did you enjoy this book? Please consider leaving a review.

Reviews help us authors sell books so we can afford to write more of them. Writing a review is the best way to ensure that the author writes the next one as it lets them know readers are enjoying their work and want more. Plus, it makes the author feel warm and fuzzy inside, and who doesn't want that? ;)

ABOUT THE AUTHOR

JASMINE WALT. She a NYT bestseller who is obsessed with books, chocolate, and sharp objects. Somehow, those three things melded together in her head and transformed into a desire to write, usually fantastical stuff with a healthy dose of action and romance. Her characters are a little (okay, a lot) on the snarky side, and they swear, but they mean well. Even the villains sometimes.

When she isn't chained to her keyboard, you can find her practicing her triangle choke on the jujitsu mat, spending time with her family, or binge-watching superhero shows on Netflix.

Want to check out Jasmine's other books? You can do so at www.jasminewalt.com. She loves hearing from her readers, so drop her a line anytime at jasmine@jasminewalt.com.

ALSO BY JASMINE WALT

The Dragon's Gift Trilogy

Dragon's Gift

Dragon's Blood

Dragon's Curse

Dragon Riders of Elantia

Call of the Dragon

Flight of the Dragon

Might of the Dragon

War of the Dragon

Test of the Dragon

Secret of the Dragon

The Baine Chronicles Series:

Burned by Magic

Bound by Magic

Hunted by Magic

Marked by Magic

Betrayed by Magic

Deceived by Magic

Scorched by Magic

Fugitive by Magic

Claimed by Magic

Saved by Magic

Taken by Magic

Tested by Magic (Novella)

Forsaken by Magic (Novella)

Called by Magic (Novella)

Her Dark Protectors

Written with Emily Goodwin

Cursed by Night

Kissed by Night

Hidden by Night

Broken by Night

Printed in the USA
CPSIA information can be obtained
at www.ICGtesting.com
LVHW090807200624
783441LV00004B/15